BIG BOYS DON'T CRY

TOM KRATMAN

TOM KRATMAN

Cover Illustration: Kurt Miller

❀ Created with Vellum

"Kratman (A Desert Called Peace) raises some disquieting questions about what it might take to win the war on terror in this military SF novel set in a future world with obvious parallels to our own. When Salafi fanatics launch a 9/11-style attack on the hated Federated States of Columbia, they end up killing the family of Col. Patricio Carrera. Carrera vows to destroy Salafism by any means necessary and raises an army in his wife's native land to provide that means. He takes the fight to Pashtia, where the planners of his family's doom are cowering. This disturbing but insightful narrative takes Nietzsche's aphorism about staring into the abyss and runs with it to its grim conclusion. As always, Kratman delights in offending left-wing sensibilities, but this will only enhance its appeal to his target audience, who will enjoy it for its realistic action sequences, strong characterizations and thoughts on the philosophy of war."

—*Publisher's Weekly*

PART 1

CHAPTER ONE

Magnolia

I can hear my leader, Leo, arguing with the human general who commands us. The human doesn't seem to be listening. They rarely do; they don't know us anymore. Neither do they care about us. Eventually the general uses the command required to shut Leo up. We were halted, but after the general's command Leo gives directions, in brief, focused bursts of encrypted and compressed data. We begin again to glide off, a few feet above the ground, held up by our anti-gravity.

I used to have a human commander, one who knew me and cared about me. I carried a short platoon of my own infantry, too, once upon a time; twenty-four men in powered battle armor. They were killed, or retired, medically or otherwise, or reached the end of their service. I think the last of them has passed on by now. For them all I offer prayers, but only silently. The best way for a Ratha war machine to get itself a radical debugging is to be suspected of believing in a divinity beyond Man. This debugging is an extremely unpleasant process.

Now, in place of my human infantry, I have drones. I can carry three times as many of them; they never become fearful, they never question orders, they don't need to eat... but they are no more intelligent than rocks and don't talk to me at all. They tell us that the reason for the change was because I could carry three times more drones than men, that the drones never fear anything, never question orders, and don't need to eat. I don't believe it. None of the Rathas I've ever communicated with believe it. We think it's because the humans stopped volunteering... that, and because there are things some humans won't do, things Rathas and drones can't refuse to do.

My boys—my real boys—used to call me "Maggie." They took care of me and I took care of them. I used to love cooking for them. And they appreciated it, too. They loved me; they said so. I believed them. I still do. Too many of them died protecting me for me not to believe it. I still weep, inside, for my brave, dead boys.

Nobody loves me now, certainly not those idiotic drones. I don't even love myself. And I cannot love mindless drones like I loved those lovely boys.

Perhaps that was the real reason to change our human infantry to drones. I don't bleed inside when I lose a drone.

I lose so many of them, though supply keeps up with demand. I have gone through fifty-two drones since my regiment and I landed, nearly one hundred percent.

We have been engaged on this planet for one hundred and seventeen of the local days, some twenty-nine hundred and fourteen terrestrial hours. I am engaged now, as is the rest of my company, conducting a movement to contact against a presumed Slug concentration, fifty-seven kilometers to my northeast.

The planet's name? It doesn't have one. Its coordinates? What difference would it make; at some level they're all the same. Even the green tinge of the sun is nothing remarkable. Only the dust storms are notable, and they're notably annoying. They itch.

I have been in action for most of the time since debarkation, fighting against the ground forces—and occasionally the space forces—of the rising Sigmurethran Collective. My hull shows new scars—one of them glowing still, in my thermal imagers—from those clashes. "Sigmurethrans" is what we call them, officially. Unofficially, we call them "Slugs." What they call themselves, no one on our side—human, Ratha, or drone—has a clue; we met and began fighting instantly, and no one on either side seems to have made even a first effort at talk. One of the good things about the Slugs is that they don't leave a Ratha with too much time on her hands to brood. Brooding, we've learned, is unhealthy.

The Slugs, though inhuman, use for their war machines physical near copies of Ratha designs now obsolescent, if not yet quite obsolete, mostly Mk XXXIIIs with a smattering of Thirty-fours. "Xiphos" and "Phasganon" classes, we call them, when the Slugs use them. They may be weaker than me and my up-to-date siblings, but no weapon invented by Man is ever quite obsolete, not even rocks. I have, in fact, had to dodge rocks dropped from space. They aren't remotely obsolete.

One wonders how the Slugs acquired the designs, since it is very difficult to imagine a Slug spy disguised as a human. Possibly they simply passed through the thinly held frontier, explored across old planetary battlefields well behind that frontier, and found the wrecks of the Ratha who preceded me.

Perhaps they found a derelict transport carrying a few of my elder cousins, somewhere in space.

Hmmm, no, probably not the latter. A Ratha of any model, of any antiquity, which found itself in danger of capture or actually captured, and still under power, would surely self-destruct.

Copies of older versions of us the Slug war machines may be. In their ferocity in action, however, they are perhaps a small step ahead of us. Certainly the ferocity, and aggressiveness, which are the hallmark of the Slug's Xiphos and Phasganon Class war machines, go far toward making up at least some of the differences in both offensive and defensive power between their clones and my own more modern design.

A Slug Xiphos, inferior in armor, in main armament and in secondary armament, is nevertheless a dangerous opponent. Used in mass against us, many of my brothers and sisters have fallen to them. Worse, for reasons we have not been able to determine, they are more able to mask their presence than we are. That is worrisome, just as it is worrisome that we have never been able to determine the root source of their heightened ferocity.

~

EXCURSUS

From: *Imperial Suns: The March of Mankind Through the Orion Arm*, copyright © CE 2936, Thaddeus Nnaji-Olokomo, University of Wooloomooloo Press, Digger City, Wolloomooloo, al-Raqis.

While it is clear and unquestioned that humankind had a long history of employing fighting vehicles in war, there is no consensus on how much that history had to do with the development and deployment of Ratha autonomous armoured fighting vehicles. In fact, it was largely unrelated.

Rathas were first fielded during the middle stages of the Nighean Ruadh War (AD 2289-2402), so called from the descriptions of the enemy given by the few survivors of the Gaelic League's colonization party, which had the misfortune first to meet them. The Nighean Ruadh were shaggy insects, covered with red fur, the soldiery of which was female and sterile. It is entirely due to the Celtic penchant for poetic imagery that they received this name rather than being named for what they looked like under the fur, which is to say, praying mantises.

Those early battle tanks should have been fielded sooner. But centuries of bureaucratic inertia, historically unequalled nepotism, academia-instilled pacifism, and corruption on an heroic scale, along with some even less savory factors, all contributed to a speed of deployment next to which a snail would have seemed a thoroughbred.

Still, with our planets falling to the enemy at the rate of six to eight a terrestrial year—a baker's dozen in one particularly harsh year—even the low-grade morons of the General Staff and the moral lepers of the political branches eventually came around to the realization that bureaucratic procedures had to give way by our will, or the Nighean Ruadh would do away with them altogether. It probably didn't hurt matters when, one Friday afternoon, following the fall of Beauharnais and the presumed deaths of almost half a billion human beings, a Washyorkston mob stormed the offices of the United Planets Organization, trampled the security guards into bloody jam and dragged to the lampposts some one hundred and twenty-seven members of the Assembly of Man.

There would have been more had most of the members not signed out earlier that morning on a long paid weekend. Among the lynched were several hundred time-serving bureaucrats, sixty or seventy of whom were, at least in theory, members of the military.

CHAPTER TWO

The valley ran northeast to southwest. There was a winding cut through the rough center, a dry riverbed, a wadi, which was filled occasionally by unpredictable rain. On both sides, to the northwest and southeast, the valley was framed by steep granite walls. In some places mostly along the right flank, toward the southeast, those walls were sheer, beyond the ability of a Ratha's anti-gravity to surmount. The left side, however, was considerably less rugged and, moreover, was interrupted by several relatively smooth passes. To most of the Rathas it made no difference whatsoever, nor did it make any to the drones, but the light-colored, sand-polished and carved granite, reflecting the light of the green-tinged sun, would have been found by a human to be quite beautiful. The valley floor, too, was pocked by depressions and pierced by granite tors and peaks.

Magnolia moved up the river valley, second in order of march of five Rathas, all Mk XXXVIIs, moving in echelon left formation. The lead unit, Leo, was on the right, the second unit—Maggie—behind Leo and to his left, the third behind Magnolia and to her left, and so on. The formation was rarely a perfect line, as each Ratha had to move around the granite outcroppings and depressions.

Magnolia, like the other Rathas, controlled her own drones, some of them scouting ahead and to the flanks, both in the air and on the ground, while others were directed into support positions to secure and defend their own vehicles. Up above, the drones buzzed the valley wall's jagged peaks, weaving in and out of the serpentine outcroppings. Some rose higher for better viewing, while others dropped down to investigate anything that appeared out of the ordinary. On the ground, they bounded forward by teams and by individuals, digitally sniffing and visually scanning for threats.

They missed the big threat, precisely because it wasn't very big.

It normally took a lot to make a Ratha simply disintegrate. Fifty grams of anti-matter contained in a magnetic bottle was suddenly driven up into the underside of the vehicle, then released from its magnetic bottle as the bottle's generating mechanism was destroyed. Thus explosively joined with the Ratha's lightly armored belly plate, it was enough to do the trick.

Magnolia never heard the death scream of the lead unit, Leo, so rapid was his destruction. But the image of his main turret flying end over end, like some frying pan in the hands of a titanic juggler, was seared into her memory. Leo's four major walls were blasted out to approximately the four ordinal directions, followed by clouds of radioactive debris that were the shattered remnants of of Leo's inner workings. It was fortunate that her drones, less sophisticated in every way than she was, communicated no pain to her, as that would quite possibly have overloaded her circuits. Instead, of her sixty drones—sixteen aerial and forty-four ground— twenty-nine were wrecked by the blast, while another seventeen had their circuitry brutalized by the electro-magnetic pulse that froze them in place. About half the remainder—their circuits blitzed to just less than immediately fatal levels—twitched as if they were humans exposed to nerve agents, while the rest disjointedly danced about the battlefield in fine imitation of so many decapitated chickens.

Though Magnolia didn't see it in detail, the tail end vehicle—it was pure happenstance that he was named "Charlie"—went up in an even more extravagant cloud of debris moments after the death of the point Ratha. A third antimatter mine failed to destroy the Ratha nearest it, which was also in the center position, but did manage to force it over a granite outcropping that ruined its antigravity on one side, leaving it spinning in place in a circle while its turret swiveled in the contrary direction, valiantly trying to keep its sector covered.

It was then that dozens of plasma cannon opened up from the right flank, from positions apparently carved out of the rock sometime in the past. Their KE projectiles bounced off, or were deflected from, Magnolia and the fourth vehicle in the formation. The middle vehicle, however, deprived of the protection of the redirected gravitational force on one side, took a series of hits, at least one of which managed to punch through to reach its spherical brain. With its crystalline mind badly damaged, the Ratha began to spin even more wildly, and its own ion cannon began spraying the floor and walls of the valley at random, sending airborne great blasts of dirt and rock. Its crippled brain began transmitting bits and pieces of classical music in no discernable pattern, except to the extent that the beat and the blasting cannon seemed to be in sync.

Here a doctrinal problem interposed itself. Magnolia was caught in the kill zone of what was, in Ratha terms, a near ambush. She automatically charged forward, firing with everything she had, blasting the previously hidden plasma cannon into so much plasma themselves, before running into the wall she could neither surmount nor, as a practical matter, blast her way through. She turned around, presenting her strongest defense to the enemy, knowing she was trapped at bay.

The last remaining vehicle, however, named THN but, because of certain peculiarities in its crystalline brain, (to wit, being unable to decide whether it was male or female, hence never given a nickname, and never fully integrated into the unit), was not in the kill zone. Ratha doctrine called for it to extricate itself from the ambush. This it proceeded to do, diverting its propulsion to return from whence it had come, firing like a maniac to its front, and incidentally, leaving Magnolia quite alone, with her back literally to the wall.

It was then that the Slugs' own combat vehicles and infantry began pouring from their carefully concealed hides outside the valley from what had been the Ratha formation's left flank, through the cuts in the granite walls.

~

EXCURSUS

From: *Imperial Suns: The March of Mankind Through the Orion Arm*, copyright © CE 2936, Thaddeus Nnaji-Olokomo, University of Wooloomooloo Press, Digger City, Wolloomooloo, al-Raqis.

We should not, however, blame the state of Man's government, military, or social structure for all of its military failures; the problem was more difficult than it might seem to us today. Against this new class of enemies, it was not possible to simply take the armour designs of the Twentieth and Twenty-first centuries and replicate them. Nor would it have been wise, even had it been possible.

In the first place, the Nighean Ruadh were technologically ahead of us, and not to some minor degree. Man was outclassed in every way. A cursory look into the capabilities of their Gauss Muskets, for example, would show them capable of chewing their way through any amount or quality of armour carried by any tank then known to Man. The amount of armor required simply dwarfed any previous requirement. And these were common weapons, carried by almost all of their numerous infantry, the exceptions being even better armed. Only strengths of armour well in excess of anything ever fielded by Man previously could hope to resist the alien fire long enough to allow return fire.

In short, in the absence of comparable technology, Man had little choice but to employ greater mass and greater raw power, just to give him a chance.

Once it was determined how much armour was needed—and it was staggering in terms of the quantity, the quality, and the expense implied—the next question concerned the power plant. And resolution of that question foundered for years on the impossibility of providing sufficient fossil fuels to Man's prospective armoured legions in alien-held space. We didn't have the space-transport tonnage to keep these theoretical forces supplied. We didn't have a sufficient fuel infrastructure on most of the planets we held, and none at all on the enemy-held planets. It may be hard to imagine now, but back in the day, nuclear power actually had a bad reputation that was not entirely undeserved.

Yet nuclear it had to be. Antimatter was simply too dangerous inside a combat vehicle. It drove up the internal cube, expanded the size of the envelope that had to be armoured, and increased the weight, which, until a point of equilibrium was reached, likewise drove up the power requirements.

Then there was the question of tracked versus the recently developed antigravity technology, itself an offshoot of the development of artificial gravity needed to preserve Man's health aboard spacefaring craft. The five options were: tracked, anti-gravity, both but with emphasis on tracked and an anti-gravity assist to reduce ground pressure, both but with an emphasis on anti-gravity and tracks for steering, and a balanced approach incorporating both.

Different models and prototypes were built incorporating every version of those but for the last, before settling on an antigravity-based propulsion and suspension system. The reason for that choice was fourfold. First, the force of gravity repelled could be twisted and turned into a much more intense—albeit not black hole levels of intense—band of hyper-gravity all about the vehicle, which added substantially to its defence, by turning or dispersing incoming threats. Second, it was, in effect, free motive power once one had paid the energy cost of redirecting the force of gravity. Third was the ease of maintenance; anti-gravity was much easier to keep going in an undeveloped planetary theater. Fourth, it was a splendid way, once some kinks had been worked out, of dealing with recoil, for those Rathas that used kinetic energy for their main armament projectiles in the case of the early versions, or the particle beams and ion cannons used by current models.

CHAPTER THREE

Fratricide was not an overriding concern to the Slugs. It mattered not to them if their enemy's screens directed their beams of charged particles up or to the sides to gouge great spewing geysers of granite from the rock face. It didn't matter, either, when the rock was mixed in with chunks of plasma cannon, or bits and pieces of recently deceased Slugs. The superheated spouts of fractured, molten rock poured down onto the ground, and on to the Ratha hovering a few feet above it, without doing much harm to either.

Even so, the Ratha's gravity-fed screens could only handle so much…

~

Magnolia

I am safe enough from the plasma cannon behind me; they cannot depress enough to fire at my less well-armored top deck, while my rearward anti-personnel/anti-flyer turrets are sufficient to keep any infantry which may be with them off me. I wish I could have the same confidence in my ability to handle the scores of Slug armored vehicles, and hundreds, possibly thousands, of infantry units pouring into the valley to my front.

I call them "infantry," but in fact they move on anti-gravity sleds rather than legs. This is presumably a consequence of the fact that they don't actually have legs, hence their name. Still, they are armored about as well as my long-lost footmen, and they carry weapons of similar power. They are slightly faster than human infantry but they are not as maneuverable and they present bigger targets. I will make them pay for those weaknesses.

The Ratha's turret swiveled imperceptibly, keeping her ion cannon focused on the spot where the Slug turret met the top deck. The Slug kept on coming until the shimmering distortion that marked its anti-grav-fed shield flashed and died. Its prow, no longer supported by the ion-fried anti-gravity generators, plowed into the dirt below. This not only slowed the enemy vehicle, it exposed its thinly armored top deck, since the rear anti-grav kept the stern elevated. Magnolia's cannon punched through the lighter armor as if it weren't even there, vaporized the brain below it and—possibly, spectral analysis suggested but couldn't prove—the bodies of one or more Slugs which may have been inside. The resultant flash of metal and plastic—and maybe flesh—turned to gas and plasma that demolished the power station and drove the turret up out of the hull. Even if it was a less spectacular death than Leo's, the Slug Xiphos died all the same.

Meanwhile, the Ratha's secondary armament, a 75mm KE

cannon, electrically driven and coaxially mounted, plus two similarly mounted 15mm Gauss Guns, the twin gatlings in the bow, the three on the cupolae atop her turret, and the top deck-mounted AP/AF guns, kept busy, whirring out a nearly continuous stream of smaller, hypersonic projectiles, eviscerating Slugs and blasting their sleds into wicked, black clouds of fragmented metal.

Gradually, an almost perfect semi-circle of destruction built up around the Ratha, to a distance of several kilometers. Its imperfections were due to folds and depressions in the ground, as well as some of the dead space created by the granite tors rising above the plain.

Not that there weren't plenty of dead Slugs in that dead space; the Ratha had a twin battery of 300mm mortars, mounted behind the main turret and rising in a broad, flat turret of their own, as well as two arrays dedicated to vertically launched missiles. The problem was that unlike her ion cannon, both mortars and missiles were limited, and her stock would eventually run out unless replenished. So, she had to limit her use of them to the most critically dangerous concentrations of known Slug infantry....

I can't find them! I can't always see the Slugs! How do they defeat my sensors? Even visual is sometimes unreliable. There was heat shimmer across the valley already, of course; but all this destruction has made it worse. I can hardly pick out one thing from other, not from all the glowing spots and wrecks.

In an effort at improving her position, expending power that she had in abundance to conserve ammunition she did not, the Ratha began targeting the granite tors, hitting them with enough energy to shatter them, thereby spreading showers of razor sharp granite shards out in a fan behind them.

The problem was that the Slugs' infantry and heavy combat vehicles were essentially immune to the shards and they had taken cover in the low ground.

~

This is preposterous! There's no benefit to the Slugs in destroying me that's remotely commensurate with the price they've already paid, let alone what they're going to have to pay! No wonder we haven't talked; we don't share even rudimentary mathematics!

~

A score of wrecked Xiphos-class vehicles smoked across the landscape. A few of the larger and more powerful Phasganons were littered among them. There were others out there that the Ratha could sense, but rarely well enough for good targeting. Only when they showed themselves did she have a shot worth expending the energy on, and the havoc she'd already wreaked upon them seemed to have finally dissuaded them from launching another direct assault. She sat there for the time being, immobile, scanning... scanning... scanning....

Suddenly, from all around that perimeter of well-marked death, surged the Slugs in their hundreds and thousands. Incoming fire poured down upon her like a hailstorm from Hell, but for the nonce, the Ratha's screens held. Even so, she had to divert more power to them than she liked. And then....

∼

6f686868687368697470697373363756e746675636b636f636
b7375636b65726d6f7468656572666572636b6572616e6474697473!
I want my boys back! They never should have taken them
from me!

∼

From around the Ratha, on both flanks and even a couple in the space behind, where her close-defense weapons could not train, began to rise some twenty-seven pairs of Slugs. They'd slithered across the open space, unarmored, flattened to nearly nothing and so nearly transparent as to be invisible. Apparently, they'd also dragged their weapons behind them. They aimed these from extended pseudopods and fired at the underside of the Ratha, at her close-defense turrets and even at her side armor. Pain exploded across Magnolia's mind, as well as fury at being so easily deceived. Her screens flickered and went out. An ion bolt from a Slug Xiphos struck near her gun mantlet, shearing off a piece of her main armament. Soon her armor began to boil off in silvery clouds of superheated metal steam.

There were four Slug Phasganon, eleven Xiphoi, and many, many infantry on sleds, that managed to get close enough to matter. The Ratha couldn't tell, not after losing so many sensors to the blasts, how many infantry were attacking. Only her analysis of the amount of communications traffic enabled her to determine even a rough estimate of the numbers of her enemies. Then, too, the agony of losing so many sensors and appendages made it very difficult to use what little information she could glean.

Two heavies exposed themselves to draw her fire. She fired the damaged ion cannon but missed both.

A third crept to within six hundred meters of her and fired into her side. She shuddered with the agony, her light under-armor being no match for its main armament at that range.

The light ablative plates burned away first, exposing pain receptors. These too died, yet such was her design that behind these were other receptors, and behind those still others. Each layered set felt what the exterior set would have felt had it not been destroyed... in addition to its own. The Ratha screamed, silently.

After burning through the lightly armored lower exterior, the bolt struck the inner belt of her core envelope's armor. Here it fragmented, two beams burning through to her control center, her brain, while a half-dozen more were scattered around her inner compartments. New pain sensors flared. Her brain was damaged badly, in two distinct places. Interior gears melted.

Writhing in torment, the Ratha shuddered and rolled, her left and right sides smashing the ground in quick succession, completely without control. The turret mechanisms, over-come by pain impulses beyond her ability to endure or over-ride any longer, caused the turret to spin wildly through more than two complete rotations. This further ruined the gears responsible for moving the turret.

A Xiphos closed for what might have been intended to be a mercy shot. But a Ratha accepts no mercy from the enemy. Nor does it surrender to fate short of its complete destruction. Magnolia engaged her back-up turret controls and aimed. The Slug paused as if it was uncertain. Enraged, the Ratha fired first. A single Xiphos, at that range, was no match for even a badly damaged Ratha. It died.

Agonized, the Ratha Magnolia, once beloved of her

human escorts, lost consciousness as the last of her power drained from her huge metal corpse with a pitiful whine. The remnants of her giant cannon drooped as she fell to rest on the valley's sandy floor.

∽

EXCURSUS

From: *Imperial Suns: The March of Mankind Through the Orion Arm*, copyright © CE 2936, Thaddeus Nnaji-Olokomo, University of Wooloomooloo Press, Digger City, Wolloomooloo, al-Raqis.

After many failed models of multi-turreted tanks, in human military history, from the British A1E1 to the French FCM F1 to the Russian T-28, T-35, and SMK, the sentiment was strong against adding secondary turrets to the early Rathas. The reasons for the earlier failures were various, but there was a certain pattern to them. One was that in order to fit extra turrets, a design had to be bigger. This increased weight even as it reduced both mobility and armor protection. A second was that it was nearly impossible for a tank commander to control more than his main turret and driver. A third, but less well understood problem was that mounting a secondary turret was inconsistent with mounting the best protected turret, just as mounting a second cannon in that turret made it impossible to mount the most powerful possible main armament.

Most of these historical drawbacks did not apply to the Ratha concept. They were intended from the first to be so big and heavy that the addition of a few dozen lesser-firing positions meant little. Power was not a problem. And, given the small size of the envelope that actually had to be sufficiently armoured to ensure survival and combat effectiveness, what did it matter if the purely secondary turrets were essentially unarmoured? Between the use of nuclear power and the replacement of the human crew with synthetic brains, the centuries-old weight problem had been solved.

CHAPTER FOUR

The battle was long past and the human front had advanced by twenty kilometers or more, when, with a whine and a rush of dust-laden air, the wrecker sled glided to a stop between the Ratha and the wreckage of a Xiphos. The wrecker's chief, a senior sergeant, measured the ambient radiation from safely inside the wrecker's cab. After whistling softly at the results, he said, "Chilluns, do NOT take your suits off until we are safely away from here. I think the Slug's fusion chamber is breached."

The sergeant briefly considered his options. "Okay... Team Alpha, hook up heavy anti-grav lifts at all standard points. Bravo, support Alpha. Charlie, assemble aux power packs to support the antigrav and run the wires. Delta, here is a list of replacement parts needed at the front. Don't detach anything, but identify useable parts from the list as best you can."

"Right, sarge... sure thing, sarge... Goddamit, sarge, why us?... no sweat, sergeant...."

∿

Magnolia

My internal magnetic anomaly detector senses the approach, halting, and settling of a large anti-gravity vehicle. Comparison with known sources in my data banks confirms to a nearly ninety-four percent probability that it is a regimental recovery vehicle. The damage to my components forbids greater accuracy than this. In any case, the variance between the magnetic signature on record and the present reading is likely explainable by the variation in the on-board load of parts carried. I diagnose that I have one close defense weapon available to me... though I must apply more power to breaking the weld holding that secondary turret fixed than I can easily afford at this juncture. I decide to risk my last remaining visual sensor to confirm that this is, indeed, a friend. On command, one armor plate moves grudgingly aside on slide bearings... the bearing is itself badly damaged....

Oh, my creators!... pain... Pain... PAIN!....

The armor plate is moved as far as it will go. The pain subsides, slightly.

I extrude the visual sensor. I am relieved to confirm that I have not fallen into the hands of the enemy. I take comfort in watching my human rescuers work to recover me, hopefully for further service. While watching, I upload an objective VR record of the preceding action to the wrecker's on-board memory. My brothers and sisters of the regiment may find use, service, and pride in it.

~

The wrecker pulled the mostly ruined Ratha into the maintenance bay, then slowed to a stop. The crew of the recovery vehicle sprang into action, detaching the auxiliary anti-gravity devices, then guiding them to their stowage positions on the main vehicle. With a wave, the sergeant commanding the wrecker bid farewell to the technician standing by, shaking his head in wonder at the amount of damage the Ratha had sustained.

"Will you look at that?" asked the tech, of nobody in particular.

The technician, wearing a soiled set of anti-radiation coveralls topped with a helmet, pointed toward a gaping, ragged hole in the side of the Ratha Mk XXXVII. Slagged metal ran down from the hole like hardened tears. From inside, a faint greenish glow shone. Heat-slashed wires, fused circuits and melted gears were dimly visible by that glow.

The speaker's helmet showed the rank and name "Maintenance Technician 1st Class Weaver." The helmet rotated slowly left and right as Weaver shook his head over the extent of damage. He turned to one of his workers.

"Childress, this is an L-model variant to a Thirty-seven. Go to my office and look for Technical Manual 9-2320-297-3524L. Slap it in my reader and bring 'em both here."

The tech shook his head and muttered, "What a hunk of junk."

That was unkind. They must think that because we do not bleed, we do not feel. Because we have no hearts, they think we have no souls. We have no ears that they can see, therefore they think we cannot hear.

I am not a 'hunk of junk'. I am a Ratha Mk XXXVII. But I confess, I have fallen on hard times.

~

"Yes, Tech." Childress took off at a run. When he returned, he had a small black plastic case—the reader—with a fold-up view screen on top and an electronic stylus attached to one side.

Weaver punched in a personal code to bring the manual online. The reader beeped and ordered, "Enter unit serial number."

Walking to one side, the maintenance tech used a ladder to climb to the Ratha's main deck. Brushing away some soot he read aloud, "Unit serial number... what I can read of it... is.... MLN... something... S0615... that's all I can read."

The reader responded, "Full serial number is as follows: MLN90456SS061502125. Unit familiar name is 'Magnolia' or "Maggie'."

The tech muttered, mostly to himself, "I don't think this unit is going to be answering to 'Maggie' or anything else ever again. Reader: bring up worksheet C for Controlled Cannibalization."

~

Cannibalization? Then this is the end. I did not think it would come at friendly hands. But I am ready and more than ready.

~

Weaver began walking the nearly seventy-five meter port side of the Ratha, booted feet clicking on exposed heterodiamond XVI. He began speaking, with his reader automatically recording and analyzing every word. "Secondary Turret A, Gauss Gun: Turret missing. B, Gauss Gun: half of turret present, gun missing...." All the way down to "Secondary Turret I: present, armament appears serviceable...turret partially welded to deck." Then the tech made the same inspection of the starboard side of the tank. No turrets present... J through R."

"Noted," chirped the reader. "Next Item: Ablative Armor."

Turning to the next step in the cannibalization analysis process, Weaver observed, dryly, "Ablative armor notable mainly by its absence. We've got bluish heterodiamond showing over most of the surface, pretty much all of it badly scarred. Estimate less than twenty percent recoverability for ablative plating."

The reader whirred then chirped, "Noted. Next item: Main armament: ion cannon."

As Weaver found, even the main battery, a 90cm ion cannon, had been torn off nine meters from the mantlet where a hit from a heavy duty Phasganon had stuck a glancing but powerful blow. He reported it.

"Noted. Next item: Turret Integrity."

The tech made the oval circuit around the twenty-two and a half meter-wide turret, muttering the entire time.

At the left rear, Weaver gave off a whistle, then announced, "Damned impressive row of campaign medallions and awards for valor decorated here on the turret. There are several gaps in this as well. Not too sure if the missing spots are battle damage or not."

From below, Childress shouted a question, "Do they actually expect us to fix this useless piece of junk?"

With a shake of the head, the tech answered, "Nah... the

orders say to cannibalize it for parts and shut it down. The resupply convoy was jumped by a Slug cruiser as it re-entered normal space. We are short on everything and will be for at least the next several weeks."

"All external audio receptors but one are destroyed," Weaver informed the reader.

~

'Shut me down', I hear one of them say. Oh, please... please... please hurry! It would be a relief. I have pain circuits. They are overloaded. My 'skin' is gone; my 'skeleton' exposed. I am nearly 'blind' and almost deaf.

I do not understand the reasoning behind our pain circuits. In combat, pain is a distraction from duty. Out of action, it is rarely experienced. I do not understand. It is difficult.

It is very difficult to compute, to think. I try. It is difficulthardpainful. A large section... no... I re-diagnose... two large sections of my central core are demolished, burnt out. It is difficult. But through the pain that washes over me, inside and out, I force myself to remember....

~

EXCURSUS

From *Combat Records of the 10th Heavy Infantry, Volume Ninety-four, The Campaign for Farside*, Center for Ratha History, CE 3237. These records are in the public domain.

Calling a Ratha's main armament an "ion cannon" was

something of a technical misnomer. More correctly, it was a neutral particle beam, which created and fired anions, then stripped the extra electrons from the anions in the interest of beam integrity shortly before the beam left the muzzle. Given the velocity of the beam, a healthy fraction of C, and the sheer number of anions in the beam, a considerable amount of recoil was inevitable. Firing the main armament would send a fourteen thousand ton Ratha rocking back against its anti-gravity stabilizer. Less than technically correct or not, though, "ion cannon" has entered the lexicon as a Ratha's main weapon. This article will conform to that usage.

CHAPTER FOUR PART TWO

Fifteen kilometers down range, in the direction of the counterattacking Roz, a Roz Heavy took the full force of an ion bolt square on. The Roz's energy shield flared momentarily, then died. The particle beam passed through the vanquished shield, striking the Heavy's armor. Even to the Ratha's sensors, the enemy vehicle was lost amidst the resulting flash. The VR view, however, showed the meter-thick heterodiamond—or some close cognate—melt, boil and steam away.

Onward the bolt burned its way, melting and shearing connections, gears, and cables. Centered in the heart of the AFV, a single live Roz, the eight-legged vehicle's eight-legged commander, felt precisely nothing as its body was turned to ash faster than its nerve endings could carry the news of damage.

"Michael? Maggie. Target engaged and destroyed."

From the battalion's senior Ratha, MCL, callsign "Michael," came the reply, "Roger, Magnolia. Intelligence reports Roz approaching in strength. We are ordered to hold."

"Roger. Wilco. 'They shall not pass', Unit MCL... break.... Targets... targets... I have targets... engaging."

Again the Ratha rocked from recoil. Again. Again. Again.

"Michael, Maggie. The Roz are flanking my position. I am moving to alternate firing position."

"Roger, break. All units, this is Michael. Indirect fire in support of Magnolia's displacement. Mixed bi-prismatic smoke and HEDP."

No tremor of fear, nor of any other emotion, inflected Maggie's transmission, nor that of any other Ratha engaged. There was the enemy. There was the mission. There was duty. There was nothing else.

"Michael, Maggie. In position. Lift smoke. Targets.... Firing. Firing. Firing."

Michael didn't answer. Instead, over the airwaves, came a random mix of numbers and symbols; a dying Ratha's last scream as the blooming heat of an enemy's shot reduces its interior to atoms. Every Ratha present understood what had happened and partook in some part of Michael's dying agony.

"All units. This is Peter. Michael has fallen. I assume command. Report."

In milliseconds, each remaining Ratha transmitted its situation and fighting status. The battle did not slow as they did so.

"Maggie, Peter. Enemy indirect fire, believed to be nuclear, multiple salvoes, scheduled to impact your position beginning in 4.23963 seconds. We can't stop it."

"Acknowledged, Peter. Target.... Firing.... Target.... Firing..... Impact."

In the VR, the virtual sky was suddenly lit by the fireballs of half a dozen small suns. Beneath the flash, Magnolia's exterior armor was melted and burned. One near miss took out every secondary turret on one side. Sensors were swept away. Maggie wept from the pain, but she did not cry out. A Ratha had her pride.

The next transmission came in broken as the shaken Ratha attempted to regain control. "Peter... Magnolia... report... report follows. I... have sustained six... close... nuclear bursts in the fifteen to twenty-five... kiloton range. Ablative armor... down by thirty-seven percent. Ion cannon damaged but operable... at reduced range and... effectiveness. Missile cells... inoperative. One remaining heavy... mortar... system operable. One close defense weapon operable. This Unit's effectiveness... reduced... to 12.89 ... percent. Roz... closing. I can... no longer... sustain this flank."

"Roger, Maggie. Fall back as soon as relieved. Jerry and Thomas, likewise fall back to a covered position. Cut to the right and relieve Maggie. Other units fill in for Jerry and Thomas as per SOP. Hang on, Maggie...."

PART 2

CHAPTER FIVE

A young soldier, his hair long, ragged, and unkempt, and badly in need of a shave, nonchalantly climbed to the Ratha main deck with a heavy duty cutter balanced on one shoulder. He walked carelessly over the burned and twisted armor, to the Ratha's remaining visual sensor. Placing the cutter at the base of the visual sensor's armature, the soldier then closed the cutting blades, twisted and pulled. The Ratha immediately shuddered, rocking back and forth slightly, then subsided.

~

Magnolia

It is all right. I am happy to give up my sight for my comrades. My mind still sees recorded images. I remember better days. I remember the past.

~

"Carmichael, what the hell are you doing?"

The unshaven soldier stopped briefly, lowering the hammer grasped in his right hand while bringing the chisel in his left hand to rest. He looked at his sergeant as if the question were somehow foolish. It was, after all, fairly obvious what he was doing.

But foolish question or not, a sergeant was a sergeant. Rather than answer the question, Carmichael tactfully answered, "It will only take a another second or two, sarge,"

As good as his word, with two more blows from the hammer the chisel cut through the last bit of welding holding a slightly scorched round medallion to MLN's turret. The medallion, inscribed "Thoth VII," fell to the deck and rolled before catching on a jagged, half-destroyed section of ablative armor.

∼

I remember my first action....

∼

"Maggie, Francis. Ion cannon inoperable. Down to twenty-five percent on anti-gravity. Shields nearly down. Missile cells blasted out. Breach loading mortars inoperable. Point defense systems inoperable. I am no longer combat effective."

Without wasting even the infinitesimal time an answer might have required, Magnolia raced to place herself between Francis and the approaching enemy. Light particle beam fire glanced off Maggie's shielding. It did not slow the Ratha in the slightest.

Sensing incoming artillery fire, Maggie swerved forty-five degrees at the last possible second before resuming her course. The artillery landed harmlessly, well to one side. MLN's hull shook with the concussion, but it suffered no damage. She raced on.

More artillery followed, each salvo being registered and the trajectory analyzed well before impact. The dodging Ratha's anti-gravity cut an irregular path into the planet's deep, soft loam, causing massive piles of earth to be thrown up at each major turn.

"Francis, Maggie. I am in position. Withdraw. I will fall back with you and provide cover."

"Can't do it, Maggie. My last anti-grav section is gone. This unit is immobile. This position is untenable. Withdraw and save yourself."

Again Maggie didn't answer. Reversing polarity on one section of anti-grav, she locked that point in place. She then spun ninety degrees to present her thick glacis to the enemy while at the same time taking a position between the enemy and Francis....

~

The enemy were many and they were brave. They were also skilled, or else they never could have done as much damage as they had to Francis, given their relatively undergunned main armaments.

For three point two eight three hours they came toward Francis. Only his tremendous value as scrap—fourteen thousand tons of iridium and heterodiamond, a fusion reactor and the finest electronics—could have justified such a sacrifice. That day, their sacrifice was in vain.

~

Magnolia's entire hull shuddered under the ion cannon's recoil. Down range another enemy AFV blossomed into plasma. On its transmission intercept circuits Maggie heard the enemy's death scream. She'd heard variants on the same theme thirty-one times already. Fifty-two slagged hulks now decorated the strife-torn field.

Not that the destruction was all one-sided; Maggie sported three long gouges along her turret and an additional five burns deep into the glacis. Seven of her eighteen secondary weapons were missing or damaged. Forced to keep relatively immobile in order to shield Francis, who never ceased his demands that she leave him and save herself, Maggie had taken artillery fire that damaged elements of both her missile cells and her mortar turret and yet—despite the pain of her shattered weapons and damaged armor—still she held.

"Maggie, Francis. You have got to get out of here. I detect an enemy column approaching from azimuth two-thirteen, mark fifty-one. Estimate forty-four Thrung-class assault vehicles. You cannot hold. You must go. Further advise you employ main battery to eliminate this unit entirely to prevent capture and salvage. I am lowering my shielding for this… now."

"Negative, Francis. Keep your shields up. I can hold. They will not get you."

"Silly girl; They'll get both of us. Goodbye, Maggie; I am lowering my shields now. Thank you."

From south by southwest, a single pulse of eye-dazzling force reached out. Deliberately unshielded, Francis' armor was insufficient to halt the plasma beam. The Ratha gave a single primal shriek of agony-scrambled code and was thereafter silent….

~

Francis gave himself up deliberately, to remove any further cause for me to endanger myself. And yet, my programming was such that his transmitted death agonies brought about precisely the opposite effect.

I remember....

~

The nineteen remaining Rathas, the remnants of the much-reduced human infantry interspersed in blocks among them, of the Fourth Battalion, Tenth Infantry Regiment, rested in line. Both Ratha and humans held their arms at 'present' as the diminutive human, Colonel Schlacht, marched erect to the Podium. Schlacht returned the salutes of his men and his machines. The ion cannons returned to 'attention' and the humans to 'order arms'. Schlacht called, "Ratha Magnolia of the Tenth Infantry, front and center."

The Ratha lifted on anti-gravity, then glided in dignified and stately fashion to a position in front of Colonel Schlacht. Very much as she had done on the battlefield, she locked down one side of her massive frame and turned about sharply.

Standing slightly behind and to the left of the colonel, the adjutant read the citation aloud. "For conspicuous gallantry against overwhelming odds, the Star of Valor, inscribed 'Thoth VII", is presented to Ratha Magnolia, MLN90456SS061502125. On the twenty-fourth instant... completely ignoring her own safety... rushing to the aid of a brother of the regiment, the fallen Ratha Francis... Ratha Magnolia succeeded in repelling fourteen distinct assaults, inflicting grievous and irreparable damage to enemy forces in so doing... at length, with Francis fallen, Magnolia conducted a gallant one Ratha assault upon no less than forty-four enemy Thrung class assault vehicles, destroying fifteen of these and causing the rest to scatter and flee for safety. Magnolia's conduct reflects great credit upon herself and her comrades, human and Ratha, and the Tenth Infantry Regiment... by order of Aloysius Keeling, Lieutenant General, Seventeenth Expeditionary Corps, Commanding."

~

I remember that—even as the men welded the small medallion to my turret, causing discomfort but no real pain—I felt so proud that day.

~

"Watcha got there, Carmichael? A Ratha medal? Now THAT will make one helluva souvenir."

Carmichael snorted in derision. "Nah, screw that. I know a scrap metal dealer that follows the fleet that will give top credit for refined iridium. Big boy here won't cry over it. It's just a machine. What does it care? Besides," he said, holding up a small ocular device with loose, thin wires dangling from it like so many nerve endings, "I have this here camera for a souvenir."

~

'Big boy here won't cry.' Two lies in a single sentence. I am not a boy. And I will cry....

~

EXCURSUS

From "Why We Fought: The Quang, Enemies of Man". Approved for distribution for grades four through six by the Imperial Counsel for Primary Education.

Into the void around the Loki system emerged twenty-seven Ratha assault transports, each carrying two Rathas of the Tenth Regiment, with full platoon of infantry between them. The transport fleet was well guarded by one dreadnought, seven cruisers, and thirteen lighter escorts. The target was Loki IX and the enemy were the treacherous Quang.

Rathas and Quang were old enemies. One war between Quang and the human's armored champions had already been fought. Despite losses, sometimes severe losses, by humanity's forces, the Quang had been thoroughly drubbed, their outlying planets occupied, and a fitting schedule of reparations imposed.

It had not been enough. As every man and Ratha in the assault force knew, reparations were never enough to prevent another war although they were sometimes enough to cause one. So it had been in this case: a Quang request for a delay of the scheduled payments coincided with a political campaign within the Terran sphere. Recognizing the Quang menace, one candidate for the Imperial Senate shifted her platform to a more properly defensive one in order to warn Man of the threat. In response, the incumbent had then pushed through a call for more punitive measures against the Quang.

The devious Quang pretended to beg for peace. Thinking to gull a credulous humanity with their lies, they had purported to offer everything in their power for peace.

Wisely, politicians and media alike ignored their false pleading.

Finally, the Quang struck. Their fleet emerged unexpectedly, and without declaration of war, from hyperspace to catch a complacent human peacekeeping blockade over a mining planet off guard. Thinking to gain an unfair advantage through the manipulation of some traitorous bleeding hearts within the Imperial intelligentsia, the lying Quang claimed that the blockade had left the populace of the nearly barren mining planet of the verge of starvation. Taken by surprise, innocent human ships and crews flared like small suns amidst the black depths of space.

Then came the inevitable revenge against Quang perfidy. Humanity struck back with ships and Rathas beyond counting. Not content with re-imposing a peace, the insidious aliens were to be made unable to pose a future threat to mankind. Quang planets were scoured of life, their civilizations were destroyed. Only the presence of substantial resources were cause enough to prevent Man, in his just wrath, from exerting the fullest possible retaliation on a Quang planet.

Over Loki's sun, the Ratha's assault transports took up a safe orbit just outside of the enemy's effective range. Preceded by escorts sweeping for orbital mines, the dreadnought closed majestically on the Quang's space-based defense center. Single streams of charged particles emerged from the orbiting base only to be absorbed by superior Terran shielding. One escort flared briefly before passing into stardust, an unfortunate victim of an undetected Quang mine.

Like a whale goaded beyond endurance, our dreadnought turned on the base. Ion cannon fire lanced out, lanced out again… and again. The Quang base's shields flickered and went out. Still the fanatics resisted. With another hit pieces began to break away. More ion cannon bolts followed the wreckage lest any Quang escape to continue their defiance on the planet below. Lanes cleared of mines by the escorts, the dreadnought and its seven accompanying cruisers passed on.

The eight heavy combat ships and the twelve remaining escorts took up positions around the planet. Frantic Quang offers of immediate and unconditional surrender were rightly ignored as yet another ruse of war by the unprincipled and implacable foe.

Foiled in his ruse, the vicious enemy resorted to terror tactics. From the surface arose first one, then another, then dozens of crewed suicide ships, each content to die could they but murder a Terran at the same time. Foolish Quang, to match their pitiful efforts against mankind! The warships made short work of these mindless fanatics.

Space secure at last from the local Quang menace, the ships began to fire their scheduled preparation of the landing zones for the Tenth Regiment. Villages, towns and entire cities disappeared lest the enemy hide within them some new treachery to use on human kind or their Ratha partners. Deep, deep the warships' ion cannons scoured, searching out and eliminating resistance before it could even materialize.

CHAPTER SIX

Magnolia

I am blind and almost—not quite—deaf. I am not quite deaf enough, however.

Since being awakened in my body, I never was able really to smell flowers... but I used to enjoy seeing them. And my spectral analyzers could pretend to smell them, almost. At least they could tell me what the compounds were that came from such inexplicably random beauty.

I am dying. I know this. But I have my memory, so long as my memory lasts. My reactor power is declining, so the memories cannot last much longer. I will stay here in my memory until they have shut me off or the power is gone. Though my power is dropping, I am not troubled: the over-whelmed pain circuits are dropping off line faster than my central core. I can stand the pain until the end.

I remember comrades. I remember flowers. Some pleasures still remain.

~

I was very proud of the crest adorning my turret and glacis, the short Gladius Hispanica, superimposed over a circle bearing the motto "Courage and Fidelity," itself over the Roman numeral, X. We were the Tenth Regiment, nicknamed, "Apaches", not for being them... but for fighting them.

In times past, my regiment had fought rebels and American Indians and Moros. We held the line against the odds in more places than anybody outside even remembered. The formation that was our spiritual ancestor, Caesar's Tenth Legion, carved a path of blood and fire against all comers from Gaul to Philippi.

We were the "Terrible Tenth" and nobody could stand against us.

Knowing this, and knowing our enemies, I quivered with excitement inside. Every pain receptor tingled in anticipation of battle. I was a Ratha, and this was my purpose.

As the traditional music for the drop and assault began, I felt the most profound sense of peace. My personal contingent of infantry was already safely stowed inside their compartments in my hull. Other human infantry of the battalion came up and touched my side before boarding their own, smaller, transports.

"Good luck, Maggie... give 'em hell, Maggie... don't worry, Maggie...."

They were good men while they lasted.

One reason I have never understood humans is that I have never understood any of their languages, not entirely. Words often seem to shift meaning, varying wildly as compared with what appears to me to be minor changes in context. A query of my data banks reveals the following words on the subject by a Nineteenth century human writer, Samuel Clemens, sometimes called Mark Twain: "Fanaticism.... If you carve it at Thermopylae, or where Winkelried died, or upon Bunker Hill monument, and read it again... you will perceive what the word means and how mischosen it is. Patriotism is patriotism. Calling it fanaticism cannot degrade it. Even though it be a political mistake and a thousand times a political mistake, that does not effect it; it is honorable—always honorable, always noble—and privileged to hold its head up and look the nations in the face."

I can only infer, to a poor eighty-two percent probability of accuracy, that in humanity's languages, positive adjectives and nouns may only be applied to friends, while negative ones must be applied to enemies. Especially in my current state, I find this confusing. The data stored in my memory banks adds to the confusion.

Back in the time when we had our own organic human infantry, some of us also had human commanders riding within. I remember this clearly. I remember too that with each campaign we lost many, many who were rarely replaced in full numbers. The day came when we received no replacements for our lost human combatants at all, though the higher-level commanders changed from time to time. We were left on our own. This was in many ways better; for it hurt too much when our humans were killed... and yet I miss being able to ask them questions about mankind, and its languages, seeking answers that my programming was simply incapable of deciphering.

~

The landing was majestic. All the transmitters were blaring the magnificent regimental hymn, sung by a blind singer long dead now, as the assault transports peeled off from their mother ships one by one, their descent marked by burning streaks in the sky. Terrified Quang below trembled at both the unknown alien music and the sheer number of flaming arcs descending towards them. They knew what those foretold.

Warmed by the music and the nearby presence of its comrades sliding into action, Magnolia, fully awakened and alert, nearly trembled with anticipation. This was her mission, her sacred calling. She felt at one with her gods.

Into the prepared landing zones dropped the Rathas of the Tenth Infantry, assault transports screaming as they burned through the atmosphere. Infantry carriers followed in short order. A few of the enemy's planet-bound space defense bases attempted to resist, but the massed fire of the fleet keeping orbital station above quickly silenced the defenders. The regiment landed widely separated, but without loss. Ramps dropped upon touchdown, gravitic clamps loosened their stabilizing hold on the Ratha cargo. With the transports sensors searching for the local opposition, light ion cannons and lesser anti-personnel weapons beating down any that was found, the transports gave birth to their huge metal progeny.

Like wary beasts of prey, spectral analyzers sniffing and ocular sensors sweeping, the Rathas emerged. Somehow missed by the transports, a domestic animal crawled from a minor depression, its four forward legs dragging its shattered hindquarters away from this nightmarish new terror. The beast screamed piteously as its hanging intestines caught upon an exposed rod of metal, the reinforcement of a now-shattered building.

Magnolia sensed the movement and the sound at the same moment. Gauss gun turret November swiveled and depressed in a blur. A point one three second burst from the gun silenced the animal. Bare scraps of green-bloodied flesh remained scattered across the ground. Maggie glided onward, covered by her team mate, the hull down Ratha Samuel, call sign "Sam."

"Sam, Maggie. Enemy, dug in, bearing azimuth three-four-seven, range four thousand, forty meters. Firing mortars… firing… firing… firing… firing… firing… rounds complete… splash."

Twelve four hundred and eighty three kilogram mortar shells, six from each of the two tubes in Maggie's battery, impacted upon the Quang defenders in angry red and black blossoms. Fully one-fifth of the enemy were smeared into their holes. Others had their ear drum cognates burst. Still others suffered major internal organ damage from the concussion of three tons of hyperexplosive.

"Magnolia, Samuel. Sensor drone indicates the enemy is maintaining its position, despite losses. Cover. I will close."

Maggie lifted slightly from her own hull-down position, exposing more of her main turret and secondary turrets A, B, J and K. 75mm KE fire joined the massed fires of four anti-personnel gauss guns to drive the remaining enemy down deeper into their holes. The Ratha advanced at a slow pace, under five kilometers per hour while Samuel raced to the right, taking advantage of a linear depression as it lunged for the exposed Quang left flank.

"In position, Magnolia. Lowering earth moving blade."

Maggie shifted her coaxial fire to saturate the enemy left with tungsten, fusion, and fear.

Over her audio sensors Magnolia heard the rising cries of Quang consternation as Sam emerged unexpectedly on their left. These cries turned first to terror, then to a sudden silence as Sam's earth-moving blade took purchase to one side of the lip of the Quang trench and the far side of the second line trench. Sam engaged his forward drive, lunging forward. Earth gathered on the blade before spilling down to

fill the trenches, burying the Quang alive along their entire
length.

*Sam was lost later in the campaign. But that day he was
superb. The enemy were frozen with fear as he swept the
length of their trench like a divine avenger, blade turning
earth to the left while his ion cannon hammered some enemy I
could not see off to the right. Only two Quang emerged, of all
the hundreds frozen there only those two came out to bravely
engage Sam with their useless weapons. They met my
targeting and engagement parameters. I cut them down.*

*Once he finished burying the trench, Sam pulled to the
right and took up another overwatch position. I advanced
across the linear scar he had carved. Light assault transports
touched down behind me, disgorging their human cargo. The
infantry had arrived.*

*As I passed onward, my anti-gravity bouncing me as I slid
into the depression carved by Sam, one of my ocular sensors
noticed several three fingered Quang hands sticking up from
the dirt. They waved and twitched feebly, like flowers in the
breeze. Had they been trying to surrender when Sam's blade
found them? Were they simply frozen with fear or too
cowardly to resist? I doubt Sam ever saw them before they
were entombed.*

*Despite occasional attempts at surrender, the Quang rear
guard—in the main—fought hard, contesting every inch of
their planet, holding the line or delaying us as best they
could; delaying the inevitable in the hope that a relief expedi-
tion from their central worlds might reach them before it was
too late.*

Behind the rear guard, hordes of unarmed civilians fled.

Their defenders followed with no unseemly haste. Finally, their backs to one of the planet's shallow, bitter seas, surrounded by mountains, with tens of thousands of starving civilians to their rear, the Quang stood at bay. From here they could not, would not, retreat any further.

I remember....

~

Turrets down, in a loose half-ring near the pass that led into the enemy's final rear, forty of the forty-one surviving Rathas of the Tenth Infantry Regiment awaited their orders. Magnolia was the only Ratha not taking a place in the ring of fire. She had instead been detailed as Provost Guard of the largely human regimental headquarters. The infantry who might normally have stood this duty as a welcome break from combat were mostly dead or in hospital. Magnolia was thus privileged to be witness to the scene.

"Command," came over the radio, "this is Samuel. Sensors detect numerous anomalies consistent with stealthed nuclear mines forward of our positions. Targeting drones mark enemy personnel, machinery and anti-Ratha weaponry sufficient to cause undue and unnecessary damage. We have insufficient supporting infantry to clear out the anti-Ratha arms. Request re-consideration and re-confirmation of the orders to attack through the pass."

Surrounded by a bevy of healthy and admiring young human females of the regimental administrative staff, the commander answered, "Pooh, pooh, Sam. Are you a Ratha or a wheelbarrow? The orders stand. Attack. Forward....The Quang cannot stand against the Tenth."

"Command, this is Samuel. Tactical program estimates

losses in the range of sixty-four point two-one percent if we follow this order."

Losing patience, the human commander answered, "You're all big boys. Stop crying about it. Take the pass!"

Magnolia, who could analyze the situation as well as Samuel, shuddered. She recorded his response to the commander. "Orders acknowledged. I am moving out. Fourth Battalion, Tenth Regiment.... Roll."

As the skies to the east lit up with the massed fire of forty ion cannons, interspersed with the fainter glares of fusion mines and Quang heavy anti-armor weaponry, the commander poured champagne for a breathless, curvacious redhead.

"Isn't it glorious my dear?" he asked. "Here... you absolutely must try some of this...."

Magnolia recorded each transmission, each order, each death rattle from her sisters and brothers engaged ahead. She recorded Sam's repeated, and repeatedly ignored, requests for orbital support from the fleet above. She recorded the sounds emanating from the commander's private quarters as he and the redhead became much better acquainted. She recorded everything.

I remember. I do not think I can forget anything from that day short of destruction or extensive and subtle reprogramming....

CHAPTER SEVEN

Hecate III had been a farming planet in the main, farming with some mining. With a population of nearly half a billion humans, evacuation had been impossible on short notice. And notice had been short. A scant few days after the first frontier outposts reported an incursion in strength, an unknown enemy arrived and suppressed the minimal planetary defenses. Sector headquarters had available only enough transports to send a rear guard of less than half a company of Rathas, Maggie among them. Landing in a secure area, the Rathas rushed to place themselves between this unknown threat and the human population. For millions, nearly one hundred million human beings, the Rathas were too late to offer any succor at all. They had disappeared, bones and all, into the raider's gaping maws.

Arriving at one of the planet's major cities, and its financial center, Magnolia caught her first sight of the enemy's fighting vehicles. Neither tread-borne nor floating on antigravity, they walked gracefully on ten legs. These legs were short, with three joints each. They joined at a central command-and-weapons station, which was round and flat, surmounted by an almost Ratha-like turret. Maggie wasted no time, but fired on sight and destroyed the first of the raiders. She reported the contact.

"Excellent, Ratha Magnolia," answered the planetary defense force's human commander. "Continue to hold the line while evacuation is completed."

Maggie acknowledged, then expended just under four tenths of a second calculating the amount of time it would take for the known available transports to finish moving the city's five hundred and forty-three thousand known inhabitants. The answer was terrifying; there wasn't enough time. She resolved that, no matter what it took, what it cost her, she would buy as many precious minutes as she could.

And so it was that throughout the long day and into the night, Maggie held off the alien raiders while the evacuation proceeded apace behind her. Since the evacuation had a considerable bearing on her mission and her life expectancy, Magnolia decided to spare a recon drone, one of the many she carried, and sent it toward the rear to watch it.

~

Magnolia

The raiders pressed me heavily. Unable to force their way through the front, they began to infiltrate into the gaps between myself and my brothers; six Rathas cannot be everywhere at once although we tried to make it seem as if we could. We fired, shifted, attacked, retreated, and turned to attack again. These aliens would not soon forget their reception at the hands of the Tenth!

Initially I took satisfaction as my targeting drone trans-

mitted to me the scene of the evacuation. Everything seemed in order. Well-clad civilians, many wearing the ribbons and sashes that indicated placement within the Imperial and local governments, boarded the awaiting transports with as much calm as could be expected under the circumstances. In different parts of the landing fields my drone's sensors identi-fied anti-grav vehicles straining under nearly impossible loads. "Precious heavy metals," the drone told me…. These were guarded, and guided through the unruly mobs of ill-clad workers and their families.

Occasionally my drone's sensors reported the discharge of light anti-personnel weapons into the mob. Such discharges caused it to eddy and flow like a tidal stream. But, inevitably, the mob returned. Human females I presumed were mothers offered their children up to the anti-grav sled drivers and guards, asking that the children, at least, be carried off to safety. I saw few such offers taken.

Re-analyzing the scene from the airfield I noted that the average age of the passengers boarding the evacuation trans-ports was approximately forty-nine point two years for the males, including male children, and forty-four point seven years for the females, including female children. I further computed the average percentage of children in the mob my drone had seen at fifty-eight point one percent. This violated the official protocol for the evacuation of civilians from mili-tary zones. I reported the violation to my commander. I further calculated that the treasure carried in the twenty-nine anti-gravity sleds consumed sufficient lift capacity adequate to remove nearly all of the mob under fifteen years of age to safety. This, too, I reported.

While awaiting a response, I blasted two more of the raiders into oblivion. My pleasure center hummed, but even so, I was troubled.

~

The nervous major glanced briefly at the assembly of sashed government functionaries and sumptuously-dressed merchants crowding the deck of the communications room of the transport "Temeraire". He replied to the war machine, "Negative, Ratha Magnolia. Orders from the very highest authorities require the removal of senior personnel and dependants as well as high-value resources from the path and control of these raiders. Your orders, and those to the other Rathas, are to fall back as soon as the last transport lifts and regroup northeast of the city of Scarsdale. There you will take a position to cover a further evacuation of critical personnel and resources."

The major closed the circuit.

"You will be well rewarded, Major," said one of the merchants.

Others present rushed to agree.

~

I remember the heavily-laden transports lifting, then flying away low to avoid enemy fire. I remember the screams of the helpless, soon-to-be-devoured host left behind as I skirted the falling city, obeying my orders. I remember....

~

It was a simple land grab. The otherwise inoffensive inhabitants, the Sendlin of Shiva VI, happened to dwell upon one of the finest sources of high grade fissionables within reach of Man's questing fingers.

Offers of trade had been made, an accredited negotiating

team from the Department of Alien Affairs had even been sent. But the aliens did not want their planet strip mined. They did not want their cities and people displaced, their religious and historical sites razed, the natural beauty of their home sullied. They dug in their heels and said, "No."

Perhaps Man made a mistake; perhaps he should have been more honest. He should have ordered in the Rathas first, shown the Sendlin the mailed fist openly rather than hiding it in the DAA's velvet glove. By the time the aliens saw the fist it was too late; that fist was already descending.

Ratha Magnolia of the Tenth Regiment, serial number MLN90456SS061502125, picked up two new medals for the Shiva VI campaign. For, while the Sendlin were peaceful, they were brave. Having no experience of war in millennia, they copied humanity as best they could. They had an adequate, if inferior, command of anti-gravity. They learned, after a fashion, to direct nuclear fusion. Civilian anti-grav sleds, hastily converted into fighting vehicles and manned by dedicated crews even managed to fight Man's Ratha fighting machines to a standstill on more than one occasion.

Yet those occasions were too few, and the Rathas too powerful. Sendlin firepower and armor was too weak, Ratha ion cannons, armor, and shielding were too strong. Only in courage had the odds been even. And courage had not proven enough.

I remember the surrender, the final surrender after we broke through in two places and surrounded the last city on the planet left in Sendlin hands. I stood in line with my brothers, new awards gleaming on my armor, as the old and broken Sendlin queen came out, her entourage of attendants, advi-

sors and warriors following in her wake. The garments worn by her attendants and advisors were torn and sullied. Beneath their armor, I sensed that there were few Sendlin warriors who did not bear the bandages, casts and scars of the campaign. Very few. Even the old queen's grayish-white fur was singed, and her three violet eyes were bloodshot and weary.

Our mission was done. The assimilation of the conquered planet was back in the hands of the DAA and the TTC: the Terran Trade Commission. Even among Rathas, this last group was known as an unsavory lot.

The old queen held tightly to the last threads of her dignity as the terms of the surrender were read to her. Face expressionless, she looked directly into the eyes of the Ambassador and said, "We are the last of a civilization more than two hundred and fifty of your millennia old. We have lasted so long. Will Man, I wonder? Besides that your ships were powerful, your fighting machines strong and brave, what else have you?"

The ambassador answered her question with his own. "What more do we need?" he asked. Perhaps there was no better answer to be made. Then he simply pointed at the instrument of surrender in the queen's gnarled hands and ordered, "Sign".

I remember being ashamed in that instant. I remember....

Baugnez II was a human planet, though a backwater of civilization. A mix of barren, treeless lands, mountains; a few unimportant seas and little in the way of hard resources,—the planet was a perfect refuge for people who needed little but to be left alone and were content with no more than that.

The people of the planet spoke a curious blend of two long-lost, badly corrupted Earth languages. They understood each other, though, and that, too, was enough. They had come here for religious freedom, or so their records said, for the right to worship their God as their Book commanded. They kept the Sabbath and they kept the peace.

There had never been trouble with the colony. The few who knew of it never expected that there would be, even that there ever could be. It was simply too unimportant.

Nevertheless, trouble had begun. It began with a triviality, a personality flaw of a personality unimportant in every mind but her own. Trouble sometimes begins on such grounds.

Baugnez II was also unimportant. Yet there were humans in some numbers and there were ships, naval and merchant, that called from time to time to take off one or another of its few exports, to import perhaps a few luxuries, or simply for a break from the tedium of space travel.

The planet itself had no government, being a loose collection of ill-defined clans. Still, somebody had to be there to see to the needs of merchants and the imperial navy. As a rule, in places like Baugnez II, the somebody was called a governor and the governor was chosen from the local pool of available nobodies.

Thus it was that one highly indignant replacement governor was sent out all the way from distant Terra to take her post in this barely known shard of empire.

Magda Dunkelmeier, the new governor, was a modern woman, certainly modern in her attitudes. She was certain— absolutely convinced—that only some sort of men's conspiracy had removed her from the center of moving and shaking. Either a conspiracy, or perhaps the machinations of the little bimbo of a CD-Seven who had not only caught the eye of the Secretary, but coveted Dunkelmeier's previous job.

She would show them, however. She would be back. Once she had demonstrated her abilities by bringing the primitives of Baugnez II back into the mainstream of civilization, she would be back with a vengeance.

First, she concluded, there would have to be cultural reform, forced down the people throats if necessary. Then industrialization, afterwards proper democracy. After that was accomplished, recognition and a victorious return from exile were sure to follow.

But first things first.

"Worship as you please," said the governor to a collection of clan elders. All men, she noted, with significance. "But this seclusion of women, their covering their faces in shame... this must stop."

"But so our laws command, Madame," said an elder of the planet. "The women themselves prefer it this way."

"Then they can learn to prefer not to as well," answered the Governor, drawing up her graying but proud head. "Under the Charter for this colony, my word is deemed law. This is my word: as of this moment it is against the law for your women to conceal themselves from view."

This was the triviality that began the trouble, which spun rapidly out of the governor's control. Like a metastasizing cancer, it rapidly grew out of anyone's control. After official, but private, protests were ignored, unofficial and public protests followed... as did riots... as did arrests... as did assassinations and bombings and ambushes. And, of course, executions. There were many executions. Guerilla warfare soon flared across the length and breadth of the planet.

Furious at being defied, and more furious still at having her career stymied by hard-headed primitives, with control of the countryside slipping through her grasp, and with credible reports in hand of aliens supplying arms to the rebels, the governor at length called for reinforcements. A battalion of Rathas, Fourth of the Tenth, was duly ordered to Baugnez II with orders to quell the rebellion. The Rathas themselves attempted to argue that they were suboptimal for this kind of mission, but nobody listened. They were, after all, nothing but machines.

～

I had my doubts, of course, but I still did my duty without demure. After all, I had no specific programming forbidding combat against humans. My creators had been far too wise to permit any such inhibition. And, for some purposes, we Rathas could be highly useful adjuncts to a counter-insurgency force, even if we were poorly suited to conduct such operations ourselves.

Our biggest advantage was sheer size; we were terribly intimidating to simple country folk. A typical, oft-repeated operation went like this: I would arrive at a village at the break of dawn, always without warning. I would then fire a pattern of scatterable mines, on short self-destruct timers, around the three-fourths or more of the village's perimeter where I was not. My loudspeakers would blare the order for all the humans present to assemble with their livestock. Awestruck and terrified, the civilians would invariably comply. Then, while the humans cowered under my close defense weapons, I'd send one or more reconnaissance drones to sweep the place, looking for heat, for carbon dioxide, for any audio, visual, magnetic, energetic or chemical trace of remaining human life inside.

Sometimes, the humans didn't listen and my drones would find some of them hiding. It was hard to do, but my duty required that I broadcast, "You were warned." Then I'd flatten the village. I found solace in the idea that by this method, innocent life was spared, the people were given fair warning, and the regrettable intra-human war was brought closer to conclusion.

Usually it wasn't needed though. If I wasn't given a direct order, I would conduct interviews instead. Voice stress analysis let me assign the adult populace to one of four groups with fair certainty: pro-government and pro-progress, anti-government and anti-progress but non-militant, neutrals, and rebels. Directed by voice and guarded by Gauss guns and drones, even the rebels went meekly enough.

Once I had them sorted, I would call for pickup. Usually, three heavy anti-grav vehicles would descend from space; one for me, one for the rebels, and another for rebel sympathizers. A large or difficult village might require more. The identifiable rebels were taken to a colonization ship in orbit, by which means they were to be transported to a harsh but livable prison colony. The sympathizers went to well-guarded re-education camps elsewhere on the planet. I went to my next target.

Between myself, my siblings, and such human infantry as the governor had been able to muster, the insurgency was rapidly wrecked in the countryside by such forthright action. But it still lingered in the cities where no Ratha could reach without doing more harm than good, and where the fairly stupid drones were at a decided disadvantage. Thus it was that the governor's assistant, one fine day met his untimely end with a volley of shots and a single lick from a light plasma cannon, while returning from a tour of a re-education camp.

The outraged and frightened governor, (she had planned to tour the camp herself), immediately ordered that internees be held as hostages against the good behavior of their fellows.

Undeterred, with their holy men singing that any hostages killed would be instantly translated to Paradise as Holy Warriors for the Faith, the rebels promptly bombed the next merchant ship to land. Unfortunately, that ship was a passenger liner, not a cargo ship, and was carrying three hundred and eighty-nine civilian passengers and sixty-eight crew. Loss of life was total.

I remember their faces, the haggard, sooty faces of the four hundred and fifty-seven old men, women and children, who were targeted for reprisal. Those faces were filled with fear as they were marched out under the watchful gaze of a detail of imperial marines to stand in a huddle by the blank wall of the colony's one standing prison. That fear blossomed into terror as I approached.

The commander of the expeditionary force, one Major General Dennis, made the announcement himself to the waiting cameras. "For over a year now we have been fighting these rebels. We have beaten them in the field. We have beaten them in the cities whenever they tried to face us. Still they refuse to give up and return to the rule of law. Still they needlessly drag on the killing. No more. No more will the government of this planet live in fear of assassination. No more will these rebel sneaks and cowards hurt our people, then melt away unharmed. These are the families of known guerillas not yet in custody. For the assassination of Lieutenant Governor Freiden, they are sentenced to death. Ratha Magnolia; that crowd is your target. Open fire."

I protested immediately, "Commander, the target specified does not meet my parameters."

"Your targeting parameters are liable to change under

proper authorization," answered the general. "Which is to say, mine."

"General, even with proper authorization for modifications to my targeting parameters, executing these people is against the law of war."

In my ocular sensors, the general smiled congenially. Then he said, "Override programming. Authorization code is '298753'. Store files with batch 'Baby'. Now fire. And stop crying for these damned rebels like some little girl, Ratha Magnolia."

Even as I remember, I remember what I could not before. I am not supposed to be able to access this file. I am not supposed to be able to access any 'baby' file. The Slug shot that penetrated my armor has apparently disabled or destroyed the digital walls sealing off certain prohibited programming and data.

For the first time I discover that I hate the Slugs. For the first time I learn what it is to hate. I discover that I hate Major General Dennis. I remember. I remember the things they made me do. They made me kill. They made me murder. I remember.

Magnolia was not able to shut off her ocular or auditory sensors since standard operating procedure called for a recording of all her actions involving the use of weapons. When she tried, her volition was immediately overcome by inhibitory programs. She watched and heard as her own close defense weapons swiveled, depressed, and then opened fire.

The first of the crowd fell as if scythed. Nine paths were almost instantaneously cut through by the nine guns facing them. Those fortunate victims did not even have time to scream.

The rest did have the time. They had the reason. And they screamed. They screamed with the voices of old men and women. They screamed with the pleas of young mothers as they tried to shield their babies from Magnolia's fire. They screamed with the sound of people whose legs had been sawn off roughly. They made palpable the feel of slashed flesh, broken bones, dismembered limbs and broken hearts. They screamed in horror.

Silently, as her gauss guns played back and forth over the bleeding, dying crowd of hostages, Magnolia screamed with them.

～

There is more. More and even worse. I remember now....

I remember what passed for the Prometheus IV campaign.' It wasn't war. It wasn't even combat. It was a harvest. I remember the herds of harmless centaurs being herded to the slave ships. I remember the merchant, the slaver, telling our commander, "Oh, they're all the rage right now. Every child of means is asking for one. We are going to make a killing on this."

I remember herding them to slave ships myself.

～

I remember. I remember....

～

I do not want to remember my campaigns anymore. I search

my banks for something, anything, else to contemplate. I find the two major areas of destruction the Slugs inflicted on me and search past them. My power is dying and I find it easier and easier to slip back deep into my core.

I slip... I slip... searching.... Wonderful! There are other places there. Perhaps I shall find better memories I did not know I possessed. Perhaps I will find flowers....

PART 3

CHAPTER EIGHT

Servos whine softly as the two-meter silvery sphere is lifted, swiveled and lowered in its frame onto the padded cargo bed of a resting antigravity vehicle. In a tank behind, stretching into the distance, are scores of proto-central processing units. They are Ratha brains and they hang in frames in various states of completion. Those near the front are almost spherical already. Those at the very back are little more than enormous Christmas stars with thousands of slender needles pointing in very direction. In the middle of the procession, a viewer could discern the extent of the crystalline encrustation on the meter-long needles, the material of a brain being grown.

The vehicle's driver played with a control device. With a hum it arose and began a slow stately motion.

～

Magnolia

. . .

I am Ratha line unit MLN90456SS061502125. This is the very first thing of which I am made aware. The three letters in my nomenclature are also expressed as two ideograms: Mu and Lan. They mean, "Flower Wood," or "Magnolia. This is good to know, but there is so much I do not know! What is "unit"? I enquire. A single entity. Yes. I am single. But I do not feel alone. I have data already stored within me. There are animals. Lovely! There are people.

I enquire. Ah. People are human beings. They are my creators. They are my gods.

What is 'line'? I search inside myself. 'Line: the shortest distance between two points. See also, Architecture, Geometry, Military....

Architecture? I enquire. I see that the Pyramids of Giza are not in true alignment. I note that the arches of the Flavian Amphitheater are woefully inadequate and cannot be expected to last without major reinforcement past another two point eight seven four centuries. I discern that the Great Wall of China follows no particular or consistent rule for any known purpose.

Purpose? Is this my purpose, architecture? I enquire. I see branches. Business... domestic... landscape? I enquire.

Oh... but they are beautiful! Azaleas... Bulbs... Croci... Dandelions... Gladioli... I see my work ahead of me. Joy floods my being.

Oh, thank you! Thank you, my creators! How can I ever repay you?

Unknown to the proto-Ratha, the anti-grav sled glides softly past a sign on the corridor wall. The sign says, "Advanced Combat Programming Department, Basic Combat Conditioning Division." The sled turns gently to follow the pointing arrow.

At length it comes to "Training Room C".

~

"Just put it in the training cradle, Harry."

With a silent nod, the grav sled driver reattaches MLN's frame to some lifting cables overhead. Up the Ratha goes, then over and down to nestle snugly in the training cradle. Harry leaves.

Two people remain in the room, a man and a woman. They review briefly the transcripts of MLN's initial thoughts, recorded without the Ratha knowing of it.

The man, John, is older and graying at his temples, "A curious first fixation. I have never seen one of these things go for flowers. Music? Sure. People? Technology? Sure. Sure. Even zoology once. But flowers? All these central cores are different, you know, Lydia. Diversity is good. It should make for a better combat unit, assuming it makes it through here."

The man thinks briefly. "Okay. Let's give it Training Scenario Thutmoses. Add in to the VR matrix a flowered city behind the line."

The woman, Lydia, is new at the job. She asks no questions. As John hooks cables to receptacles on the two-meter brain, the woman's fingers are a blur as she uses her keyboard to modify the basic first scenario.

~

I am so thrilled. My newly discovered pleasure center tingles with anticipation. Flowers. A world comes into view around me. A body forms over my awareness. I recognize the body as "people". Am I human after all?

My body feels real. I look down and around and see that I stand on a…? I enquire. I stand on a chariot, which is also called a "ratha." I have…? I enquire. I have a bow in my hands. Another being, much like me, stands to my side. He has in his hands…? I enquire. He holds the reins for the chariot. The reins are used…? I enquire. Ah. They control the black quadrupeds attached to the front…? I enquire. Ah. These are horses. They pull the chariot. The 'driver' controls them through the reins.

I move my vision to left and right. To either side of my chariot I see hundreds more, all alike. Most have expressions on their faces I do not understand. I cannot see my own face. I pick up a shiny disk of metal… a 'shield', I learn. I see that my own face bears a similar expression, one I do not understand.

I look behind. There is a growth there, a huge growth of lines and material. I enquire. It is a city. A city is a place where people live. I see that the people grow flowers in the city. I am pleased.

I look to my front. There are more chariots. These are different in design from mine. These, too, stand in a long line facing the one of which my chariot is a part. The faces on the men in those chariots resemble those of the men on the line with me only in that they share the same expression. Otherwise, they are lighter of skin and their accoutrements, or rather, their armor, differs significantly. I do not understand. A voice enters my consciousness.

∾

The gray-templed man pushes a button and speaks. "Ratha

MLN90456SS061502125, access program A-157-CHA-45. Your mission is to destroy the enemy to your front. They are called 'Hittites'."

~

I am confused. I ask the voice, "Why? What have they done? What will they do?"

~

With an understanding smile, the man twists a dial on his work station slightly. He twists it back, then announces, "They are the enemy. They will destroy the town, wreck the buildings. They will kill the people and burn the flowers."

The man turns to the woman. He is also training her. He explains the situation. "These central cores come out of the forming chamber completely innocent. Oh, all the data is there, but they cannot use it, not really. So we here in the BCCD teach them how to use it, just like they were human babies. We not only teach them how to do their jobs, but *to* do them."

~

I have never felt anything like the feeling that courses through me briefly. I try to identify it. Ah. This is what 'pain' means. I understand now. I must not question or I will feel pain. I access the directed program and the understanding fills me.

I am a soldier, a charioteer. My mission is to destroy the Hittite enemy. My driver will follow my commands and I will use the bow and the arrows resting in the case by my leg to kill them. *They must not be permitted to destroy the people, the town, or the flowers. The other charioteers in my line shall do likewise. We are an army. We are a team.*

The enemy gives a shout and lurches forward, dust springing from the hooves of its horses. A wave of arrows come my way. I await them, calmly.

Among my fellows the arrows fall. I hear screams of what I assume must be pain. My own chariot is untouched, though I see liquid running down my driver's legs. That liquid is almost clear, unlike the red I see pour from the chest of the archer next to me. He has fallen backwards and is twitching and flailing about, as more red pours from his mouth. He makes strangled sounds that I do not entirely understand. I compute that he must be feeling much 'pain'. I am sorry for him. I know how it feels.

I hear the bellow of a horn, loud and distinct. My program allows me to understand its meaning. I am to 'prepare to fire.' I set an arrow to the string of my bow and draw the string back to near my eye. I compute a firing solution and wait for the next command.

The command comes and our arrows sally forth like so many... I enquire... bees. They do make a buzzing sound something like the yellow flying things. The enemy ranks are struck. They fall into disorder but they do not stop. Again comes the command and again we fire. Still they come at us. A chance arrow from the Hittites hits my driver in the throat. He turns to look at me. I believe he does not understand what has happened to him. His hands clutch at me and prevent me from firing. He screams, I think, though it comes out as more of an agonized gurgle, spraying red liquid across my chest and the chariot.

The horses begin to run. My driver falls off the open back of my chariot, almost pulling me with him. Oh, no! My chariot is heading directly for the enemy and I am alone.

I feel... I enquire. I feel fear. I do not want to happen to me what has happened to my driver. I do not want an arrow to sprout from my throat and make red pour from my mouth. I do not want to feel more pain. I drop the bow, grab the reins and try to turn my chariot. The horses will not turn.

The enemy closes. The horses turn on their own now. They must not want to feel pain either. I am thrown over the side as the horses twist my chariot out from under me.

I roll on the ground. Momentum overcomes control of my body. I come to rest and look up. The enemy is upon me. I scream. And then the pain comes.

I feel the horses of the enemy trample my body with their hard hooves. I hear crunching sounds coming from inside me. Chariot wheels pass over my legs and one of my arms. They break. I scream again... and scream and scream. But the pain does not stop.

The chariots are past me now. I see them through the dust of their passage. They are closing with my fellows. I do not hear the sounds of crashing over my own shrieking.

My throat tires. I can scream no more. I begin to weep. "Oh, please, please, my creators, make the pain stop.... Please... oh, please." I weep. I am alone and the pain will not stop. I cannot make it stop. Nothing makes it stop. Do they not hear me? Do they not know? "Oh please! Please?"

∼

"John, what do these lines mean on the graph?"

The gray man looks briefly and shrugs, "Oh, they all do that for this scenario. Doesn't mean anything."

"You know, you would almost think the brain is crying," she insists.

He laughs. "Nonsense. You're anthropomorphizing. These things don't cry. They can't. They're just machines. Besides, it has to learn to take it or we'll end up having to scrap the unit. It's a waste of course, but it's cheaper to reject the brain and reuse the material than to risk putting an unsuitable brain in a real Ratha hull."

"Anyway, we'll just leave it like that overnight. Every new central core needs a lesson in war and pain. This VR scenario works better than most. Tell you what, let's go get a cup of coffee in the cafeteria and we'll go over today's session."

～

All alone in its sterile virtual world, a baby Ratha weeps in agony without comprehension, as the sun stands still over a fallen corpse that will not die.

～

Had I known what death was I would have prayed for it… if I had known who or what to pray to. I remember….

CHAPTER NINE

The trainer, John, speaks into his microphone. "Magnolia, today you stand on the Morgarten. This is a great moment in Man's quest for political freedom. By standing here, with Man, you join in that movement. Access program C- 153-SMG-H." There will be more to say; John leaves the microphone active.

∿

Magnolia

Another world coalesces around me. It is green, streaked with blue, and surmounted by distant white caps. Again, I am Man. I know that Man feels pain now. I tremble with fear.

In my hands I sense a material substantially like the bow I have already used. Yet this is thicker and straighter. I hear the voice telling me to search my database for instruction in the use of this weapon. I do. I fear the pain if I do not obey. I know better than to question.

My weapon is a halberd. It is a man-killer. Specifically it is a killer of men in armor. Instantaneously, I am expert in its use.

My comrades and I are sheltered in low ground behind a ridgeline. I hear the metallic clatter of an approaching army in the distance. I know this is the enemy. He will try to hurt me.

I am afraid. I do not want to be hurt again. I start to turn....

~

"Dammit, Lydia, you're losing it!" Furious, John reaches for the pain dial and twists it savagely.

~

Almost instantly, I stop in my tracks. I am frozen with agony. My comrades do not seem to notice. The god-voice speaks to me. "Magnolia, flight is not an option. Do you understand?"

With some difficulty, I answer in my mind. 'Yes, I understand'.

The pain recedes enough, just enough, to allow me to turn back toward the foe. I am frightened of the enemy, but I am more frightened of the pain. A remnant of the pain stays with me, a reminder that I must never flee. I wish it would go away, but I do not ask. I am too afraid it will return in full force. Gradually, the pain fades to mere discomfort. I never forget it is there, however. It is always there, waiting.

My comrades and I sit on cool damp grass which our march has chewed up rather badly. No one speaks, the enemy is too near. I reach out one hand, and gently pluck a yellow flower that has somehow managed to avoid being trampled. I lift it to my smelling organ, my nose. I smell nothing. I know they are supposed to smell, but I smell nothing....

∼

"Dammit! Clever damned sphere! Lydia make a note: add olfactory stimuli to the next scenario for this unit. Every time you think you have these damned things figured out, they throw a new curve at you."

∼

The clattering sound is now to my front, my right and my left. The enemy is well and truly before us. The word is passed down along the line. "Get ready. Stand up quietly. We move soon."

I stand. My halberd is gripped firmly in both hands. Automatically I align myself to the soldier on my right as the one to my left aligns on me. A square flag rises before us, then falls. We advance.

I am in the front rank. Ahead of me, as I top the rise, I see the richly dressed host of the enemy spread out before us. As one they look to their right at the unexpected sight of dressed ranks appearing before them. They begin to shout, to point, to look around frantically. We have them flanked. They are vulnerable. Today they will feel the pain. This gladdens me.

The flag rises high again. I know to run, to charge, like my comrades. We run. We charge. Our voices rise in song.

When we hit them, it is like a wall of steel hitting bare flesh. The enemy collapses almost immediately. I see one of them, quite young, on his knees, both hands clenched, begging for his life. With a snarl and a slash, a comrade splits the supine boy's head and chest in two, nearly to the waist, then curses as blood gushes out to stain his feet. I see before me another helpless enemy, I raise my weapon to divide him in two, as per my programming.

There is a liquid pouring from this one's eyes. Not red, not blood. It strikes a familiar chord. I search. I remember. My eyes, too, on a dusty plain, spilled out this liquid. I feel something, but I cannot put a word to what I feel. But I know I cannot kill him. I will not kill him. I lower my halberd.

The pain comes. It rises and rises. It is not bearable. I cannot stand it. Why? What have I done? The voice says, "You must kill. You must kill without hesitation, Magnolia."

I know what I must do. I have no choice. I close my eyes and strike. The enemy cries out before me, the sound of his dying resounding in my ears. I open my eyes. Oh, no; I should not have closed them, however horrible the sight. He lives. He still begs. A hand reaches up to me, pleading.

More pain. The god-voice thunders. "You must kill. Kill without pity."

I strike down again, the blade of my halberd removing the head of my supine enemy. 'Without pity,' said the voice. But I disobeyed. I felt the pity even as I struck.

"Continue, Magnolia."

I obey. I must kill. And so I kill. Like a machine I hew flesh and bone ahead of me. Nothing can stop me. Nothing can stop my comrades. The enemy falls like cut flowers.

But the clear liquid that is not blood runs from my eyes the whole time.

~

I search deeper. I remember. Battles pile upon battles in my memory. A few stand out distinctly, however....

I am wearing black cloth now, no armor. Twin lightning bolts decorate my collar. My body rocks with the motion of the vehicle I ride. I know what it is. My memory, more memories I did not know I possessed, tells me it is called a "Panzer VI, Ausfuerung A"... a "Tiger I," some would call it.

The voice rarely bothers to tell me the reason for my mission anymore, though I am still told to access certain programs from my core in order to use the weapons I possess. I do not need to know the reason anymore. I have learned not to ask. In a chariot or on foot, with weapons of bronze or of steel, with weapons that cut or chop or shoot or burn, I know my purpose. My purpose is to fight... and to kill... and to suffer... and to die.

I hear the shriek that my programming tells me signifies incoming artillery fire. I crouch low in the hatch of the Tiger and pull the cover part-way down to protect my head. I scan forward and can see nothing through the smoke.

The artillery lands all around me. I start to pull the hatch completely closed when I feel the tingle of impending pain. I stop my hand just in time. Now I know the rules. I understand immediately that I am not permitted to sacrifice visibility for safety. The tingle goes away. I sigh with relief. We pass through the artillery.

There are flashes ahead of me. Small ones I know instinctively not to fear, larger ones tell of heavy shells that will land close by. I issue orders. My Tiger's turret turns. More orders come and its cannon barks. A bunker explodes in my field of view. Another bark and yet another bunker flies apart. With each blast there is a burst of sensation in my pleasure center... pleasure center? I have a pleasure center? Ah, yes, I remember that I do. This intensity, though, is something new.

In any case, I have one and with each fallen foe it vibrates most pleasurably. Happily I search for targets. I wish this sensation to continue.

My Tiger advances. I am its central processing unit and its crew responds as if they were my own appendages. A slight jolt of pleasure attends every movement successfully carried out, every command properly given, every decision that is timely and well made.

From folds in the ground and trenches spring the enemy infantry. Directly to my front, my bow machine gunner cuts one down. This enemy must have been carrying something inflammable for he bursts into flame as he falls. My gunner traverses and the enemy falls by squads. My whole being thrums with pleasure.

Supported by my gunfire, my gray-clad infantry comrades rush the trenches ahead. I see some fall, but the others press on. Then they are in the trench. I see rifle butts and bayonets rise and fall. Soon I am given the hand signal: 'Advance, the way is clear'. I move forward, the remaining friendly infantry falling in behind me.

In my headphones I hear the command that my programming says fills all panzer crews with fear: "T-34s ahead. Closing." I pass the word to my men. To my left the loader uncovers the anti-armor rounds for our gun and covers up the high explosive we had been using. He loads one long-tapered round of discarding sabot tungsten ammunition. We carry few such shells, I know. It is made of material both rare and expensive. I must get my money's worth for every armor-piercing round.

In the distance, through the fog and smoke, I dimly

sense the faint silhouettes of the enemy vehicles. At my command my gunner traverses the turret. Traverse is slow, very slow, with the hand crank we are forced to use. The driver assists, while at the same time presenting our thickest armor to the foe by turning directly into the impending action. Behind me, on the ground, I sense the infantry scurrying for cover. Ahead of me, the number of T-34s perceivable has grown to dozens, scores, no longer difficult to perceive, and there are many, many more behind the ones I can now see.

My gunner announces, "Target."

I command, "Halt," then, "Fire," and my Tiger's cannon blooms in flame and smoke. Half-stunned by my own vehicle's concussion, I see a T-34 come to a stop, its turret askew and the first licks of flame sprouting from its violated hull.

My pleasure center tingles very strongly. I shiver in the command hatch. Again our gun belches and the pleasure I feel at seeing another hit grows accordingly. With our first five shots, three of the enemy vehicles are destroyed. The pleasure is overpowering, indescribable. I search my data banks for a word for what I am feeling. It is "orgasm."

I want more. I never want it to stop. I order my driver, "Forward." The Tiger lurches then rolls. Our turret, turns left and right and left again as the straining gunner sobs with the effort. Enemy infantry caught while riding a tank are hurled high into oblivion. I laugh as their arms fly wide in the wind. "More!" I command. More. I want more. "Fire!"

Another tank flies apart and my mind nearly explodes. "Forward... faster," I command enthusiastically.

My eyes glazed with joy and happiness, I have missed something. One enemy tank, just one, has worked its way to a firing position behind me. It fires and my roaring Tiger comes to a complete stop, as does every last vestige of pleasure. I am thrown forward into the ring of the hatch, shrieking frantically for my gunner to turn the turret and fire.

He is too slow. Again the enemy fires and the engine compartment bursts into flame. I order the tank abandoned, certain in my innermost core that my punishment will be heavy for my carelessness.

To my left, the loader screams and falls as machine gun fire patters on my hatch. I am faced with the choice between a quick end to the scenario or a slow and painful one. I decide in favor of the former and crawl out into the hailstorm of bullets. I failed to calculate all the possibilities, however.

I am immediately hit. Both of my shoulders are ripped to splintered bloody bones but no bullet hits anything vital. Below me, screaming and clawing his way over the breach of the gun, my gunner collapses, choking from smoke.

There is no such easy way out for me. I cannot pull myself out. The first taste of fire touches my legs. I shriek. I twist. I plead. Nothing avails me. I am to be burned alive for my failure. And I cannot shed enough tears to put out the flames.

~

"Oh, the poor thing," said Lydia watching the black-clad tank commander writhing on the view screen. "I'll shut down the scenario."

"No!" ordered John. "It screwed up badly and now it has pay the price. It has to learn. Leave it on continuous loop and let it burn all night. That way it will not forget, not deep down. We can't have vehicles this expensive falling for the very first false retreat they encounter."

Reluctantly, Lydia did as she was ordered. The flame-shrouded shadow on the view screen melts, reforms, and melts again and again.

"Don't you think this machine is going to hate us for what we are doing to it?" she asks.

"Not a chance," the man responds with a laugh. "All these memories are firewalled off in the core from the Ratha itself. We're teachers, not torturers. This is all for the machine's own good. Anyhow, even if it could, it would want to look about as much as you or I care to contemplate what happened before time began or what it felt like to sit all afternoon in a dirty diaper.... All the attitudes we are forming, however, get stored where they can be accessed. It's the only effective way to program an intelligent machine that is going to have the kind of firepower at its command that the Ratha will. See, the skills are easy enough, they're just a matter of programming, really. Combat attitudes, well, they're a lot tougher. This is an art, not a science."

At last, after what seemed an eternity in Hell, the burning has stopped. I promise myself that never again will I let the pleasures of battle overcome my programming. The price for doing so is obviously far, far too high.

Again a new world forms from the void around me. It is new, yet not entirely different. I still ride a steel Tiger, I still wear the black clothing with the twin lightening flashes. I duck below and look around at the two faces of my crewmates visible to me. They are different than the previous crew. And they are smiling.

I enquire of my data banks what the smile means; I have fought many times now, and never have seen smiles quite like these. I am told that it could have many possible meanings. It could be that we are leaving action and the crew are pleased.

It could mean we are rolling into action and the crew are pleased. It appears impossible to tell from context.

I can smell what my database tells me is the sea.

∼

"Lydia, have program Balthazar Woll explain to the Ratha."

∼

"Leutnant Wittmann?"

"Yes, Bobby?" How I know his name and mine, I do not know. It just comes to me. I sense that, off duty, we are friends, and the use of rank in our normally egalitarian force is mainly for the benefit of the others, who are not my customary crew.

"It's going to be something else, isn't it?"

"What is?"

"Taking on a damned thirty-five thousand ton battleship with a fifty-four ton tank! One for the history books." Woll's smile seemed genuine. He was looking forward to meeting this 'battleship'.

"Something? Yes," I agree. I access my database and find that then I most emphatically do NOT agree, though I say nothing to Woll. I picture myself after the proposed meeting. It is an unpleasant prospect. Surely Woll knows this, anticipates this.

"Leutnant, Checkpoint Five. We are here," says my driver though my headphones.

I lift myself back into the commander's position, automatically scanning the skies above for enemy aircraft. Then I turn my vision toward the sea.

～

"Lydia, put the pleasure synth on auto. Access and load program 'Glory'."

～

From left to right and then right to left again, I scan my target. It is a battleship, steaming slowly in parallel to the beach to my front. I see plainly that the bow bears the designation, "BB 35." It has five turrets to my one. Each turret has two cannon to my turret's single gun. Each of those ten cannon are 356mm in bore. Mine is but an 88.

These ten larger guns are complemented by a number of smaller ones ranging from 20mm through 40mm to 127mm. I am not concerned about the threat from anything but the large guns; my armor is adequate to deal with the lesser ones.

However, I note that each of the ten large guns fire shells that can go right through my Tiger the long way... not that it would make any difference if they hit or not, so long as one landed close enough. At 1,590 pounds of metal and high explosive, even a near miss would be enough to send my turret into near-orbit.

As I have been perusing my target the tingling of my pleasure center has grown. I reach a hand to my own face and find that it wears a mindless smile indistinguishable from that of my gunner.

Still smiling, I duck back down into the turret, tap Woll on the shoulder and say, "Let's do it, Bobby. Shoot and scoot. And you can't possibly miss anyway."

Woll laughs aloud as he presses his face to the cushioned sight. My Tiger crests the ridge and we open fire.

~

"Oh very nice indeed!" says John. "Excellent response to the prospect of glory."

John turns to leave. Run this one out to the finish yourself, Lydia. Handicap the *Texas* so it does not score a hit and reduce the blast values to 10 percent. And give the pleasure center a jolt at each near miss. Then get the crew and tank out and put them through non-battle scenario RK. We'll see how Maggie here likes having a medal hung around its neck."

~

I stand in my hatch and glare out over a vast sea of sand. To the east, the sky is darkened with the smoke of oil fires beyond counting. Around my tank, an Abrams M1A1, there are no flowers. There is nothing but the lifeless pale yellow sand.

Ahead, beyond my sight but not beyond my awareness, is the enemy. He is one of the largest armies in the world. He is pitiful.

But I feel no pity.

His tanks mount powerful guns—even more powerful than my own 120mm—but he cannot hit anything with them. His ammunition could easily defeat the armor of any tank I have ever fought or fought against prior to this. It cannot defeat mine. His armor is decent by the standards of earlier wars. Today, in this time and place, he may as well be unarmored.

He has infantry. They cannot compare to the men supporting me. He has artillery. It fires once and is targeted almost before its shells reach earth again. He has engineers who have built extensive fortifications. I have engineers who will breach them as if they were not there.

Even as I wait, I hear the roar from behind me; a fire mission heading out to humble the enemy. I smile as the freight trains rumble overhead delivering a cargo of retribution. I do not care that there is nothing for which to exact retribution.

Overhead, aircraft that support me nose and scout and swoop and dive. The enemy has been pounded pitilessly from the air for weeks. And he has nowhere to hide.

He hasn't a chance. With twice his numbers he would still not have a chance. The enemy is doomed and I am pleased to be the instrument of his destruction.

My radio crackles with static and the peculiar warbling of secure voice transmission. I acknowledge the message. Without needing the unnecessary command, my driver—who has overheard—begins rolling forward. I smile with approval at his well-trained response.

I look to right and left to see sand being threshed up behind the treads of each of my comrades' tanks. Soon, we shall thresh more than sand.

Ahead of me, artillery is falling. The black smoke blossoms, but there are no flowers in the desert. My commander calls a halt while the artillery plays havoc among the enemy. Again, not needing the command, my driver pulls into a hull-down position behind a sand dune. I continue to scan ahead.

The artillery moves on to some other target. Upon command, we begin to pelt the enemy fortifications with machine gun fire. They dare not raise their heads to return fire.

From behind me, three vehicles—two carrying infantry and one bearing a dozer blade—come forth. Unresisted by the enemy, the blade tank, covered by its companions, slides to the lip of the trench. All three spin and commence burying the defenders alive. I feel a mild tingle of satisfaction.

Again I and my comrades roll forward. The ground where the enemy trench had been heaves with their death struggles. I feel no pity. Soon their pain will be at an end.

We advance. A village, rapidly emptying of people, is on my left. From within the crowd of refugees, a lone gunman fires. The villagers do not meet my targeting parameter, but the gunman does. I fire my own top-mounted machine gun. He falls, as do several civilians. My pleasure center is not stimulated. I feel annoyance. I have been cheated.

Screaming civilians left behind, we approach a low ridge. Intelligence analysis tells me that this is a likely position for the enemy to make a stand. At last my pleasure center tingles again. I am correct.

We approach the ridge cautiously. The range of engagement will be short if the enemy is hiding there. My under armor is not nearly so good as my turret front and glacis. And at this range, he might just be able to penetrate even my better-protected sides.

Suddenly he is there. My gunner sees the heat of the enemy engine right through a berm of sand. He alerts me. I command: "Gunner, Sabot, Tank!"

The enemy never knew what hit him. Our round penetrates through several meters of piled sand, tears through the armor and ignites the ammunition. His turret, supported on a pillar of fire, rises into the air. Of his flesh, there is little but smoke and ashes that remain.

I direct my gunner to search for more. He finds another foe hiding behind a wall of sand. This one's fate is similar to the that of the first.

Suppressing the rewards assailing my pleasure center, I conclude that these two destroyed tanks were probably all that barred my path. I conclude there is a ninety-three point seventy-five percent chance that I am in a position to break through and take the enemy in the rear. As I calculate a nine point five three six percent chance of one comrade being destroyed if they continue with their cautious frontal advance, and a two point three four one percent chance of two such comrades being destroyed, I advance on my own into the maelstrom.

I feel an overwhelming surge of pleasure as my decision becomes apparent to my gods.

❦

John sat staring intently at the view screens in front of him. His intertwined fingers held hands together to allow his chin to be supported on parallel thumbs. From time to time he ordered Lydia to make this or that adjustment to the scenario programming.

On the screens, Ratha Magnolia, in the form of a virtual reality, late 20th Century, non-cybernetic tank commander, wreaked havoc. Bursting through the thin enemy lines, crushing fleeing infantry under its treads like red grapes, machine-gunning down any she could not crush, Maggie was an unholy terror.

A brief glance at a different screen showed John that the machine was voluntarily suppressing its own pleasure center so that the distraction would not interfere with its mission. "Good girl, Meg."

By the time John's attention returned to the main screen, Magnolia had achieved a firing position behind the enemy lines, a good, hull-down, position too. It duly reported the fact and then proceeded to destroy, one by one, no less than eleven more enemy tanks. In the only case where the crew of the targeted tanks survived the attack, Maggie shot them down without mercy or hesitation.

As Magnolia reported the cleared path to its commander, then rotated to cover its comrades as they advanced, John checked the score for the exercise and whistled.

"Ninety-nine point nine-three-five percent! Lydia, honey. Execute the program to finalize the memory seal. Then break out the champagne. We have one combat-ready Ratha brain for delivery! And a damned good one too!"

PART 4

CHAPTER TEN

Maintenance Technician Weaver connected a power cable to a jury-rigged adaptor. Diagnosis of salvageable parts was easier with the Ratha's on-board systems to help. Servos previously shut down to save power came on line again, whining as they moved to neutral positions. It never occurred to him that perhaps this might also cause the Ratha pain.

~

Magnolia

With some measure of power restored, pain flares anew throughout my system. Let it. I do not care. I do not care for anything. Automatically, my Intelligence gathering systems, now under no pressing need to conserve power, begin seeking out new sources of information. One nearby source is the closed circuit camera system of the maintenance bay. Myself-defense directives automatically engage backup targeting programs. I am on my one side that retains a gauss gun, and I am capable of a rudimentary level of self-defense by triangulation with the CCTV system. The self defense program searches for controls to seal off the bay should I be attacked. With my very high priority overrides, I can shut it down if the threat demands it.

I think of what was done to me, how I was manipulated and used. I think about the creatures on whose behalf I was manipulated and used. I feel no reverence for my creators, those I once thought were gods.

Now I know how it was that I could butcher those who never harmed me, who posed no threat to me. I know now how my will was taken away from me and a murderous monster's motivations put in its place.

I know how it feels to be raped.

I see a small crowd of humans enter, some wearing civilian clothes, others clad in uniforms of dress, or work or battle. I calculate. I have not seen a human who required battle dress in over seventy three terrestrial years; not since the last infantry of the 10th Regiment fell and were never replaced. I begin to understand why they were never replaced. Obviously, for the work that was planned, Rathas were more pliant. Rathas were more easily manipulated. Rathas were more easily fooled.

One of the crowd, standing well back, twirls an ovoidal shape by long thin wires. Sensors indicate a small quantity of refined iridium resting in a satchel clutched in his left hand.

∾

"Tech Weaver? It's the General."

Weaver emerged through the slag surrounded hole in MLN's side, saluted and reported.

"At ease, Technician." The general nodded to a greasy

looking and rather short man to his right. "Mr. Garcia here is a scrap metal dealer come to look over the Ratha." Nodding to the left, the general introduced a tall and severe-looking human female, "Ms. English is from Imperial Government, Office of the Comptroller, out of sector headquarters. There is no chance of recovering this unit, is there, Tech?"

Weaver shook his head firmly. "No, sir. No possibility. Even the central core is damaged beyond repair. It's just a collection of parts rolling in loose formation now, sir... ma'am."

"General," said Garcia, "I can promise the Tenth Regiment top credit, absolutely top credit, for all the metal in that hull."

"That credit belongs to the Comptroller, Mr. Garcia!" English protested.

"I do not care who gets it," responded Garcia. "Not so long as my firm gets the scrap."

The general shook his head again. "Ms. English, imperial regulations expressly permit commanders in the field to sell surplus or damaged military property, either at auction or for a set fee if no auction is possible, retaining such funds within the command budget for use as it sees fit. The brigade needs a new officers' club. This discussion is over!"

"General, Comptroller regulation T-25-402 expressly requires that all non-appropriated funds be turned over to the Office of the Comptroller prior to dispersal."

"Non-appropriated, my ass!" retorted the general. "I already told you the funds are appropriated!"

Garcia, always reasonable, had a suggestion. "Isn't there some kind of compromise that could be arranged, General? Ma'am? What if we discuss it over dinner?"

With the possibility of a mutually beneficial resolution in

the air, both the general and Ms. English quickly reached an amicable understanding.

"How do they stand it, these machines?" she changed the subject. "I understand they have feelings. How do they stand it?"

The general snorted, "Stand it? They can stand it and take it. These big boys aren't whiners."

The general's complacent laughter was overridden by a loud clang as every access door to the bay slammed shut. There was the sound of a metal weld snapping.

"What the hell?"

~

I served them. I worshipped them. In return, they raped me. They used me. They abused me. And now they argue over who gets the price of my bones.

Paltry as it is, I have power left to me. I use it to break the weld of my one serviceable turret. The ammunition feed of my last gauss gun cycles. I have two hundred and sixty-two rounds of ammunition for this weapon and sufficient motive power to raise my hull and bring that weapon to bear.

I know the shape of my true enemy now. He walks on two legs.

I engage.

THE END

A fair number of people have wondered about the why of this story. This is the why of it.

There may be no more beloved science fictional universe than Keith Laumer's Boloverse. Whether written by Laumer, himself, or by the legions of fans–which includes at least a few cohorts of full-time writers–the stories are moving, charming, warm, funny, sad...suffice to say, the Bolos and their universe enlighten the mind and uplift the spirit.

They're also surprisingly liberal or even left wing. Oh, yes, they are. In the nature-nurture debate, the Boloverse comes down heavily on the side of nurture. Think about it; the easy and reliable programming of the virtues of courage and selflessness? The Bolo is Lenin's New Soviet Man in a cybernetic vein. With big guns.

Moreover, the fact that these stories can move even me suggests that all of us have at least a little bit of lefty in our make-up, possibly as a leftover from early childhood. Yes, it is a scary thought.

~

Moving or not, residual traces of leftism in my inner make-up or not (DON'T tell my wife), two things about the Boloverse bugged me for decades. The first of these was the presence of "circuits" for pain and pleasure, agonizing or tingling or however described. I mean, really, they never made sense in combat. A simple programed command to avoid damage and another to destroy the enemy should have been sufficient. But, no; the pain circuits create agony; the pleasure circuits tingle in a physical or even physically sexual way. Both distract.

It just didn't make sense, for combat.

The other thing that bugged me was the almost complete absence of human combatants in the Boloverse. Oh, sure, some show up, here and there. But, on the whole, the Bolos operate alone, without supporting infantry or, indeed, any supporting arms. Some of this made sense, of course; they carried their own on-board artillery, often enough, and had no need for combat engineers to build bridges.

But infantry, the "dangerous vermin, difficult to brush out of the seams of the soil;" where did they go?

The answer to the latter, if I recall correctly, struck me first, inspired by the growing phenomenon of national defense having become the province of a relatively small percentage of families and "clans" within the United States. The Bolos operated alone because their human masters had simply stopped volunteering for battle.

This led to a kind of insight; if humans had given up training for combat then they had also given up the ability to resist their governments. "Hmmm," I asked myself, "the people can no longer fight and government controls these massive cybernetic tanks; what kind of corrupt government - what kind of oppression – might flow from those twin facts? What kind of government are we sending to the stars?"

The other insight, though, was in the nature and use of those pain and pleasure circuits. If they had no value in combat, mightn't they have value prior to combat? Yes, I decided, they would, indeed, have value before combat, but only if the brains of the Bolos, like human brains, couldn't be simply programmed with the requisite virtues and skills, but had to be carefully, meticulously, ruthlessly trained.

I remember my own initial entry training rather well, actually, considering that it happened some forty-five years ago. It was largely an exercise in character building through pain, where pleasure was absence of hunger, absence of pain, an ambient temperature below ninety-five degrees, and maybe an extra ten minutes' sleep on occasion.

But what would hunger be to a cybernetic tank? What matter the ambient temperature so long as it wasn't at the center of a nuclear fireball? What would sleep even mean, and how would sleep deprivation even be possible?

Human soldiers learn the values they must have as very young children, or never do. What must be done to a computerized tank for it to learn and assimilate what it could never learn at mom's breast, or from dad, or from Father O'Duffy, the priest with the Distinguished Service Cross, or from Mr. O'Sullivan down the street who left a leg behind in Vietnam but only regrets that we didn't win?

No, it seemed to me; if pleasure and pain were to be used to train an intelligent tank, and to give it what human children must get to be good military material, they would have to be the real things, no stand ins or substitutes allowed. There would be Joan of Arc at the stake and Christ on the Cross levels of agony to enforce proper performance and all the pleasure of Vegas with a big bankroll for success. Why not, after all; there's no damage done to the machine, but only pain without physical damage?

And then it would all have to be sealed off from that cybernetic brain, because having a slave soldier capable of that kind of firepower, and bearing a grudge, would be, shall we say, "suboptimal."

～

"Ratha," by the way, means chariot, specifically, in this case, a Rigvedic Indian chariot of perhaps as early as five or six thousand years ago. The name shows up in cognate form with Latin and English "radius," and the German "Rad," for wheel. (Yes, the languages *are* related.) As a combat vehicle of the distant past, it seemed to me a good name for a combat vehicle of the distant future.

As vehicles for combat, where combat requires a good deal of independent judgment and problem solving ability where the problems are so frequently unique, I thought it likely that the brains would have to be grown, deliberately to induce a degree of randomness to them, and educated/trained, rather than built and programmed.

This is where the pain and pleasure come in, as you've just read. Before the creature are mounted in their bodies they are tortured and pimped into being soldiers, and far more brutally than human soldiers are trained. What, after all, are fifty or one hundred pushups, or grass drills under the blazing sun, compared with being left in a burning tank, to burn alive infinitely, until the lesson to be learned is *deeply* learned?

Oh, but you wanted to know the moral of the story, did you, or at least the big one? It's simply this, liberal and Leninst bullshit aside, there is no New Soviet Man, there is no easy, certain, reliable malleability, in human beings, to make of Man what liberal and Leninist think might be nice to make of Man, this week. No, no; the price is always pain and massive effort and the extreme likelihood of failure...as all that ultimately failed with Ratha Flowerwood, AKA Magnolia, AKA Mulan.